AMISH INN MYSTERIES™

Skating
the Law

Rachael O. Phillips

Annie's®

AnniesFiction.com

Library of Congress-in-Publication Data
Skating the Law / by Rachael O. Phillips
p. cm.
I. Title
                    2017954735

AnniesFiction.com
(800) 282-6643
Amish Inn Mysteries™
Series Creator: Shari Lohner
Series Editor: Jane Haertel
Cover Illustrator: Kelley McMorris

10 11 12 13 14 | Printed in China | 9 8 7 6 5 4 3 2 1

1

Liz Eckardt surveyed her kitchen counter with dismay. Bowls of asparagus soup. A platter of roasted asparagus sandwiches. Cute little dessert cups of custard covered with green-and-white veggie ribbons that Liz guessed were also asparagus—each topped with a single red raspberry.

Sadie Schwarzentruber's artistic hand had arranged it all for the Material Girls, their quilting group. To brighten this gloomy February day, she'd used Liz's cheerful creamy-yellow breakfast dishes, pastel floral linens, and a mason jar of greenhouse daisies. All very pretty.

But Liz really, really didn't care for asparagus, pretty or not. Did the others?

"Um, did Dr. Schneider put you on a special diet, Sadie?" Liz glanced at the raised eyebrows and polite smiles of the others who had gathered at Liz's bed-and-breakfast, the Olde Mansion Inn, for lunch.

"No, but I read on the Internet last week that if you eat asparagus, you'll feel lots more energetic."

The Material Girls exchanged glances. Their seventy-something friend needed *more* energy?

Mary Ann Berne—who along with Sadie owned Sew Welcome, a sewing and quilting shop—said cautiously, "I'm glad you're eating healthy, dear—"

"I wanted all you girls to feel better too. So I looked up recipes, and they turned out really yummy, don't you think?"

Who could wipe that smile from Sadie's beaming face? Liz, Mary Ann, Opal Ringenberg, Naomi Mason, and Caitlyn Ross bravely began to serve themselves while Sadie treated them to a detailed history of asparagus and its many virtues.

Liz ladled the greenish soup into a bowl and cut in half a big sandwich oozing with melted cheese. "Still trying to lose the Christmas fat." She hoped to skip the custard, which, for all she knew, tasted like asparagus as well.

When was the last time she'd willingly avoided dessert?

"Oh, it's all low calorie," Sadie enthused. "Even the custard contains fewer calories than a salad!"

So much for avoidance.

Reluctantly, Liz took a custard cup and joined the others at her big dining table. They were talking about FebFest, an event held in Pleasant Creek every February.

"With so many strangers in town, I hope nothing else happens to our Amish friends." The lines in Opal's forehead deepened. "First, a burglary at the Klassys', then another at the Oertl farm. I heard they took mostly quilts."

Sadie's face flamed. "Those scuzzballs stole Elizabeth Klassy's wedding quilt—that lovely, white double wedding-ring one she's been working on since she was a child."

"Irreplaceable." Opal's usually prim face reddened as well. "Even if she finishes one before her wedding next fall, it won't be the same. Those two patchwork star quilts Judith Oertl inherited from her Swiss grandmother were stolen too. They were rather plain—their bishop at the time only allowed dark blues, greens, and neutrals—but she treasured them so." Opal's eyes moistened at the thought of the ninety-year-old woman's pain.

"Chief Houghton told me another robbery happened last Sunday at the Gratz farm," Mary Ann added. "No wonder he advised the other Amish to leave someone at home during church services."

"Whoever's doing this certainly seems to understand their

ways." Liz's temper rose. How could anyone victimize such peaceful, hardworking people? "I heard that whoever stole Johann Gratz's cash completely wrecked his house looking for it."

"One of my customers told me Johann's wife, Ellen, just had twins," Naomi added. "Theirs is a house full of small children and mostly elderly relatives who can't do much. Thank goodness Amity organized cleanup and helped with the babies. Otherwise, things would have been so much worse for them."

Liz and the others nodded. Amity Bassinger, an Amish version of Mary Ann in that she inevitably stepped in to assist others in need. Despite the robberies, good things *were* happening in Pleasant Creek, where people helped each other.

Liz's Boston friends had considered her crazy for giving up her life as an attorney to run a B&B in this little town in Indiana, but she'd never been happier.

Mary Ann voiced Liz's thoughts. "We shouldn't dwell so much on the negative. Let's focus on something good, something fun. What's your favorite event at FebFest?"

"This year it will be the ice skater." Caitlyn, the athlete of the group, gestured to Liz. "You're so lucky that Crystal Starling will be staying here. I can't wait to watch her perform. Those jumps! It's no surprise that she medaled at the Olympics."

Liz was looking forward to spending time with the professional skater who had been born and raised in Pleasant Creek. She turned to Opal. "Do you remember Crystal as a kid?"

A little frown crossed her face. "Not well. She was younger than my children, of course. And she was always off to some city, practicing and competing."

"Crystal jumped over barrels sometimes," Sadie reminisced. "When I was a kid, I used to do that all the time too."

The Material Girls exchanged worried glances. Later that afternoon, they were meeting others at Jaynes Lake, located behind the inn, to skate.

"You'd better focus on your bowling technique instead," Caitlyn countered. "Otherwise, I might beat you in the Frozen Turkey Bowl."

"No way!" Sadie leaped to her feet. Her wiry arm arced in a demonstration of her unconventional bowling approach. Sadie often sent her bowling balls plunking into the gutter in a regular alley, but her method worked well when she hurled a frozen turkey at the pins, as Liz recalled from the last FebFest.

"I've won four out the last five tournaments," Sadie gloated, "and I'm going to win this year."

"Oh, I don't know," Caitlyn taunted, grinning. "I'm getting better every year. Are you?"

Sadie's eyes sparked blue fire.

"I know what Liz's favorite FebFest event will be." Mary Ann changed the subject, aiming a knowing glance toward Liz. "Jackson's too, I bet. The Sweetheart Dance."

"Ooooh, yeah!"

"So romantic!"

"He's the best-looking mayor in Indiana, right, Liz?"

Liz rolled her eyes as Sadie and Caitlyn filled the air with kissing sounds. Opal intervened. "Did you finally decide on a dress, Liz?"

"It was hard." Hard, but fun. She hadn't tried on so many dresses since her high school prom. Liz pulled out her phone and showed them pictures. "I liked the white-and-gold dress, but I went with this midnight-blue satin with the rhinestones."

Heads bobbed approval. Caitlyn said, "Definitely you. Sleek. Elegant."

Dancing with Jackson's strong arms around her—what could be better? Liz blushed. Okay, it was a for-real, formal date. But it wasn't like they were an official couple or anything. She took a bite of asparagus custard to bring herself back to reality. The treat wasn't half bad.

The inn's doorbell chimed.

"That's weird. I'm not expecting anyone until three." Dashing through the inn's rotunda and foyer to open the front door, Liz nearly fell over Beans, who had decided to sleep in front of the foyer entrance. The brown-and-white bulldog opened one eye a mere slit, but for Beans, that was the equivalent of a howl of protest.

"Sorry, boy. Can you just"—Liz tapped his ample rear with her foot—"move a few inches? Please?"

The chimes rang again. Beans sighed deeply and shifted his bulk perhaps half an inch.

Pasting a smile on her face, Liz stepped over him and yanked on the door.

A pink-lipsticked, toothpaste-ad smile nearly blinded her. "Hello, Ms. Eckardt? I'm Crystal Starling."

Before Liz could answer, she found herself loaded with two gargantuan suitcases. The freezing wind blew through the still-open entrance.

"Could you carry these up to my room? And help me bring in more?" The petite blonde skater turned and hurried back toward the parking lot.

Um, hello. My name is Liz. By the way, these two bags outweigh me. Missing a snoring Beans by a hair's breadth, she lurched toward the stairway.

"Is somebody staying a month?" Naomi, peeking from the rotunda, hurried to lighten Liz's burden.

"Is that Crystal Starling?" Caitlyn followed Naomi.

"Yes. I'll introduce you when we have a minute."

"Were you expecting her this early?" Mary Ann, behind Caitlyn, frowned as if someone had trespassed on her turf.

"Well, no. But—"

"Oh, you have help." Crystal bestowed another dazzling smile from the doorway. "Good. Come on out to the car."

Watching Crystal's retreating back, Liz said, "Stay here." She grabbed her coat from a hook on the wall. "I'll bring in the other luggage."

"But we can carry it upstairs to her room. Which one?" Sadie, who had also entered the rotunda, grabbed the other suitcase.

"The Heirloom Room. Sarah and I finished cleaning it yesterday, thank heaven. That bag is super heavy," Liz objected.

"I'll take it, Sadie," Caitlyn offered.

"Hey, I lift cows for exercise." Sadie grinned, though she staggered a little as she hauled it upstairs.

After two more trips to Crystal's upscale SUV—during which she mostly supervised—her belongings were finally retrieved.

"What a *sweet* doggy. Isn't he just the cutest thing?" Crystal petted the comatose Beans while the others lugged her bags upstairs and deposited them outside her room. After registering her, Liz introduced everyone.

"I'll be happy to sign autographs," Crystal offered, and Caitlyn, though clearly somewhat annoyed at the skater's self-centeredness, jumped at the chance to obtain her signature.

Liz often took guests' pictures for the inn's album. When she asked Crystal for one, the skater lit up like a neon sign. However, finding the best pose, lighting, and "energy" for the perfect photo consumed an inordinate amount of time.

Sadie and Mary Ann returned to Sew Welcome, whose door opened into the inn's rotunda. The other Material Girls left while Liz escorted Crystal upstairs, anticipating that she'd probably need something else.

"Oh, is this it?" Crystal's smile dimmed as she glanced at the other closed doorways. "I thought my suite would be on a floor by itself."

Liz dug deep for patience. "I'm sorry if you received that impression.

Yours is the largest guest room in the inn, and all the rooms are soundproof. Also, you're my only guest for a couple of days, unless a walk-in shows up. So it should be very quiet."

"Hello?" a masculine voice called from the rotunda. "Anyone home?"

"Up here, Jackson," Liz called.

He thumped quickly up the stairs. "Oh, sorry. I didn't know you had a guest."

Liz started to introduce Crystal, but the skater's schoolgirl squeal interrupted.

She threw her arms around him. "Jackson Cross! I remember—well, how could I forget you? You were my first real crush!" Crystal giggled.

What was the right response to that? At the trapped look on his face, Liz almost giggled herself.

Gently disengaging himself, Jackson said hesitantly, "I'm sorry. You're several years younger than me—"

"Fifteen, to be exact." Her bright-pink lips puckered in a cute pout. "Are you saying you don't remember me? How could you, when I'm so unforgettable?"

Now Liz coughed to hide a laugh. When she could speak again, she smoothed information into her introduction. "I'm so privileged to have FebFest's featured skater, Crystal Starling, as a guest. I was surprised to find out she grew up right here in Pleasant Creek."

"I was Miss FebFest when I was sixteen." Crystal fluttered heavily mascaraed eyelashes at Jackson. "You drove me in a convertible in the parade, and I thought you were the handsomest guy I'd ever seen."

"So glad you could join us for the festival," Jackson said. "I'm really looking forward to seeing you skate."

He was slowly backing away from Crystal. Liz aimed a glance at the staircase, hoping Jackson would catch her hint that soon he'd be teetering at the edge.

Crystal flashed her toothpaste smile again. "Maybe we can get together and talk about old times." Given their age difference, Liz didn't think there could be much in the way of "old times" between them.

When Jackson didn't respond, she lifted her chin. "But not right now. I'm going to skate with an old friend at the lake. Verena and I haven't seen each other in years." She turned to Liz, as if suddenly remembering her existence. Crystal gave a suitcase a nudge. "Oh, would you please put all these inside the room? I've got to grab my skates and go."

With a flip of her hand and a whirl of the short skirt she wore over sparkly tights, Crystal snatched a small bag from the pile. Skimming close to Jackson, she hurried down the stairs. A door slammed.

"Interesting. I wouldn't have pegged her to be friends with an Amish woman like Verena." Jackson glanced at the pile of bags. "Looks like she's staying awhile. Want some help with those?"

Liz's tired back was protesting at the thought of moving all that luggage. "Sure."

Jackson insisted on hauling the giant bags, and the task diminished considerably.

Resting her hands on her hips, Liz thanked him. "Wow, you made that a lot easier."

"I aim to please." Jackson glanced appreciatively around the Heirloom Room. "I've always liked this one. Really nice, with lots of space. Is she expecting a friend or family?" At Liz's head shake, he quipped, "Maybe an entourage?"

"I hope not. She seems to have expected a penthouse or something. And all my rooms will be full next weekend."

"You'll be super busy. I'm glad we can have some fun before FebFest blows in."

"Me too." The local festivals, so important to Pleasant Creek's economy, meant plenty of extra work for him too.

"I dropped by to make sure you and the Material Girls could still make our skating date this evening with Miriam's family."

Liz smiled. "I don't know about them, but I'm in."

"Great." He lowered his voice. "I'm glad Crystal took off. I was afraid you were going to invite her to join us."

"I was afraid I was too." Liz chuckled. "But it all worked out. Thanks for lining up the rink."

"Glad to. Bob's a generous guy to let us use it."

Bob Lindeman, who was on vacation in Florida this week, owned property on the far side of Jaynes Lake. During winter, he allowed others to use the lighted "rink" he had designed and built on the lake near his house, as well as his nearby ice-fishing shanty.

"Think you'll enjoy skating under the stars?"

"I'll love it," she answered. "So will Miriam's kids. And Caitlyn. And Naomi. And Sadie—"

He winced. "We'll probably have to keep Sadie from breaking her neck. Or somebody else's." His gaze softened again. "But I hope we can grab a few minutes to skate together. I thought we made a pretty good couple last time."

Liz's heartbeat pounded in her ears, but she answered lightly, "We did stay together well, didn't we? Let's hope I don't trip you and send us both to the ER."

"Nope. We can't do that." Jackson shook his head firmly. "We have a date next weekend, remember?"

"You don't think dancing in a body cast would be fun?"

"I'd prefer a tux, thank you. But with you, anything's fun."

They walked to the stairs. Jackson melted her with another smile as he waved. "Gotta touch base with Mary Ann and Sadie. See you around five."

Liz wanted to double-check Crystal's bathroom to ensure she hadn't forgotten extra towels and the lovely scented soaps she'd just bought.

As she did, she let herself muse over Jackson's rugged good looks and hazel eyes.

No wonder Crystal had practically drooled over him. So did most of his female constituents.

But Jackson had asked *her* to the dance. And wanted *her* to skate with him.

Not even the prospect of harebrained games like Crack the Whip could keep this evening from being special.

2

Liz spun on her skates in a series of twirls and leaps that, she was sure, would have won a perfect ten from any figure skating judge—except for a huge *plop!* of a landing on her rear. "Oof!"

"Liz! Are you hurt?" Her Amish cousin, Miriam Borkholder, skidded to a stop beside her.

"Only my pride."

Miriam grabbed Liz's hands and, with perfect balance, pulled her to her feet. How did her cousin, wearing that long, floppy dress, manage on her skates so well?

Jackson zoomed near with similar skill, the concern on his face morphing to laughter. "I must say, you put on quite a show, Liz."

She stuck out her tongue at him, then, in the pro skater's absence, flashed a Crystal smile. "Only the best for my fans."

Actually, her hips creaked plaintively, so Liz skated back to the makeshift benches Bob had set up on the shore, Miriam and Jackson gliding on either side of her.

"I'm ready for a hot chocolate break too." Jackson poured them cupfuls of Naomi's famous beverage from one of the insulated containers she'd brought from her bakery, Sweet Everything.

"Lovely evening, isn't it?" Miriam's eyes, as always, fixed on her family, playing a lively game of tag on the ice.

Liz often had wondered what had attracted Miriam to her husband, Philip, who had always seemed honest and upright, but strict. Now, as he teased and played with his children, eyes sparkling, she caught a glimpse of the tall, dark, and handsome Amish man who had won her cousin's heart years before.

Their ski-masked teen boys, who also had dropped their reserve, shouted to each other in the Swiss dialect of the local Amish. Daughters Grace and little Keturah darted like minnows, streaking almost as fast as their brothers. They finally persuaded their mother to join them, and the sight of the family at play warmed Liz as much as the hot chocolate.

After finishing his drink, Jackson donned a ski mask too and joined in the fun.

Meanwhile, Mary Ann and Opal skated sedately on the opposite side of the rink, where Caitlyn risked a jump or two. Sadie dragged two orange plastic barrels from a row that defined that side of the rink's boundaries.

"What are you doing?" Opal called sharply.

"Just borrowing them for a little while."

"Why?" Opal demanded. "Everyone needs to know where the rink ends. The ice past them might not be safe."

"Two barrels aren't a big deal." Sadie rearranged the line.

She was right, Liz had to admit. The boundary was clear. But—

"Besides, what kind of example are you setting for these children?" Opal scolded.

"They haven't even noticed. They're too busy playing tag." Sadie rolled her eyes. "But they'll notice when I jump over these things."

"*What?*"

Sadie had to be kidding. But one look at the set of her friend's jaw told Liz she wasn't.

Mary Ann must have sensed controversy, because she skated in their direction. "What's the matter?"

Opal's mouth tightened into a line. "She thinks she's going to jump barrels."

Mary Ann didn't have to ask who "she" was. "Sadie Annette

Schwarzentruber, are you trying to end up in the hospital?"

"Don't call me that," Sadie said through gritted teeth. "And no, I won't end up in the hospital. I'll take it easy, starting with only one barrel."

Opal made a choking noise.

Jackson, with a mayor's instinct for potential snags, skidded to a stop near them. "Can I help with something?"

"Not unless you can cast a spell on these old killjoys." Sadie glared at Opal and Mary Ann. "They're afraid I'll fall and hurt myself." She stuck her hands on her hips. "I'll have you all know that I've been practicing jumping barrels on my pond the past few weeks."

Opal found her voice and turned up the volume. "With mattresses, right?"

Sadie turned her back and slid a barrel away from her critics.

"Sadie's not going to change her mind." Mary Ann pulled her phone from her parka pocket, as if already preparing to call 911. At least they had Caitlyn, an emergency room nurse, with them.

The others nodded—except for Opal, who followed Sadie, still arguing.

Jackson exhaled. "The best we can do is to limit her attempts."

Caitlyn snorted. "Good luck with that."

He skated away, veering in front of Sadie.

Jackson, what are you thinking? Liz couldn't imagine how he could keep Sadie from cracking every bone in her body.

He turned and skated backward, flashing his million-dollar smile. "Hey, Sadie, this barrel thing sounds like fun. Mind if I join you? We can have a contest—say, three attempts to jump over a barrel?"

Liz slapped her hand to her forehead. Some limitation effort. Maybe Jackson *would* dance with her in a body cast.

Caitlyn shook her head. "Maybe I can arrange for them to have hospital rooms next to each other."

"May I join in the contest?"

Philip stood at Sadie's elbow, his family clustered behind him. Everyone stood stock-still. Even Opal's rant stopped abruptly.

A slow smile spread across Sadie's face. "You're on, Phil!"

Jackson helped her slide a barrel farther out on the ice. Peter, the eldest son at home, helped his father with the other. He wanted to take his chances too.

Miriam wouldn't allow the fourteen-year-olds, her son Adam and cousin Jesse, to participate. "We must have at least two men intact to do chores tomorrow morning."

Liz tried not to stare. Her cousin's tart remark came close to a criticism—something Miriam never did in public.

But Philip, smiling into his beard, never looked her way as the jumpers talked techniques and agreed on ground rules.

Meanwhile, the women prayed. The two younger boys sulked.

"Adam, Jesse," Miriam ordered, "you two stand ready to help them up after jumps. But keep to the side."

The boys complied with considerably less scowling.

Liz held her breath while Jackson gamely took the first leap—and wiped out. He scrambled to his feet with a grin, and she breathed a sigh of relief.

Miriam managed to watch, fine features locked in an impassive expression, as Philip jumped—and landed on his feet. But her fingers wrung her coat's sleeve as Peter skated madly toward the barrel and cleared it. A tiny cry escaped her lips as her long-legged son thumped the ice on his back then slid a few yards. For a second or two, he didn't move.

Jesse and Adam reached him first, and Philip had skated halfway to his side when Peter sat up.

"Next time, lean forward more," Adam advised.

The healthy glare Peter gave his brother assured Liz that the young man was fine. Miriam, however, finally exhaled when Peter stood. He and his father skated back to the start.

Sadie swaggered up to take her turn. "Now you're gonna see some real barrel jumping!"

Onlookers stiffened. Liz's heart sank into her cold feet. Mary Ann typed 911 into her phone and poised her finger over the call button.

Sadie took off, skating faster than any septuagenarian had a right to, even if she was farm-born and -bred. She easily cleared the barrel, stumbled briefly on her landing, but righted herself and skidded to a smooth finish.

"First try!" she crowed. She cast a smug glance at Opal.

Her audience applauded.

"You've made your point," Mary Ann said. "Now let's just skate and enjoy the night."

Peter, unaccustomed to contradicting an adult, said nothing, but his indigo eyes, so like his mother's, begged Miriam not to agree with Mary Ann.

Jackson protested, "But I didn't make my first jump. I want to try at least one more time."

"Let's go another round." Philip's firm voice settled the issue.

Peter shot a glance of gratitude toward his father and skated back to the start before Miriam could object. Jackson followed.

This time, the boy cleared the barrel and landed without incident, to loud cheers and clapping.

When Jackson prepared for his second try, Liz closed her eyes. Jackson was a great sport, and he wouldn't mind so much if Philip succeeded and he didn't. But what man wanted to be beaten by a boy and an old lady?

A delighted yell from those around her told Liz her fears were groundless. Opening her eyes, she joined in their celebration. Jackson hammed it up with a flourish and a bow.

"*Now* can we call it quits?" Mary Ann gave the barrel jump participants a stern look.

No, they couldn't. Liz gritted her teeth as the group added another barrel, soaring and bumping their way through a second round.

Sadie somehow cleared three barrels, but went down on her landing. Fortunately, she slid, rather than fell. All the spectators ran to her aid.

What if she wanted to try again?

Sadie let Jackson and Philip help her to her feet. With Jackson clasping her elbow, Sadie skated slowly to a bench, grinning as loud hurrahs and shouts of "You go, girl!" rang out around Liz.

When Peter, on his third try, landed cleanly, then tangled his big feet and fell, Sadie put her fingers to her lips and whistled loud enough to be heard in the next county. "Attaboy, Peter! You've got guts!"

With the group's applause, Peter managed a smile—though he obviously had wanted to beat his dad.

Now it was down to Jackson and Philip. Liz exchanged a wry smile with Miriam, who said, "At least we will be finished with this nonsense."

Miriam couldn't hide a proud smile, though, when Philip triumphed with a perfect landing on his first try, while Jackson needed all three attempts. The children crowded around their father, chattering their admiration. Philip's earlier secret smile stretched into a big grin, though he soon quieted his kids. "Don't boast, *Kinder*. Our *Gött* does not favor pride."

Jackson congratulated him, then gratefully dropped beside Sadie on her bench while the boys pushed the barrels back to their original spots.

The others, glad to be more than spectators again, scattered across the ice—including Philip and Peter, who seemed unfazed by their athletic efforts. Soon their family, along with Liz, Naomi, and Caitlyn, were dashing around the rink, playing tag again.

Before long, Liz needed a break and turned, intending to skate back to the benches.

Sadie teased, "What's the matter—you getting old?"

Liz laughed. "Unlike you, I don't lift cows for exercise."

"Me, either." Jackson chuckled. "But I'm ready to go again. After you rest, do you think you might feel like skating with me for a few minutes?"

"Sure. As long as we don't have to jump any barrels." Liz and Jackson glided back to the rest area.

Jackson set up his phone and speakers to play music while the townsfolk skated.

He must have seen Liz glance toward her Amish relatives, because Jackson said, "Some of my playlist is upbeat, but I've avoided rock. Mostly, I've stuck with classical stuff, which I hope won't offend them."

"They're used to mixed Amish-English events." Nevertheless, Liz watched Philip nervously.

Sure enough, as strains of "The Skaters' Waltz" lilted through the night, Philip paused. Would he bundle his family into their wagon and leave?

When Grace tagged him, though, he resumed the crazy game.

Jackson's shoulders, like Liz's, relaxed. "I think we're good." He held out a hand to her.

Liz grasped it. "Let's head for that corner. Our chances for survival are better there."

They started cautiously, simply skating hand in hand. Then Jackson's right arm circled Liz's waist and he tucked her left hand in his left hand. They skimmed the ice so lightly that Liz wondered if she skated an inch above it. Back and forth, they glided to the waltz.

Please, please don't let me catch my blades in Jackson's.

But this night seemed aimed toward perfection. The moon peeked out from behind black, lacy cloud curtains, smiling down on them. Sadie and Naomi applauded from the bench. Grace and Keturah skated over to watch Liz and Jackson. The girls made pirouettes like ballerinas, long black skirts billowing in the rising wind.

Again, Liz cast a look toward Philip, but he seemed intent on chasing his younger son—too busy to be critical.

She and Jackson skated until Liz's ankles grew rubbery, but she didn't want to stop. The glow on Jackson's face suggested he didn't either.

Keturah, who had lingered in their area, saved them from the dreaded blade tangle. "I'm getting cold. May I go inside that little house?" She pointed to Bob's ice-fishing shanty.

"Of course. I wouldn't mind a break from the wind myself." Liz hugged the shivering little girl, and gestured to Grace. "You can come too, if you want."

"I'll check inside first," Jackson offered as they approached the shanty. "Raccoons or some other critter might have decided this is a four-star hotel."

"Thanks." Liz drew the curious girls away from the door. "We don't want to wrestle raccoons, do we?"

They giggled, and Liz realized more than ever how much Grace resembled Liz's late mother, who had been named Deborah Miller at birth. That resemblance had been a clue that had helped Liz in her quest to find her Amish relatives when she had first come to Pleasant Creek. Her gaze wandered out over the ice to Miriam, the closest thing she had to a sister, and to Philip and the boys.

In spite of the chilly wind, Liz suddenly felt warm from head to toe. How blessed she was in family!

"Liz?" Jackson said quietly.

She followed his pointing finger and examined the old lock that hung, useless, from a splintered, rickety staple. "What on earth?"

"Smart raccoons," Jackson joked, but his grin faded as he waved the girls back and turned on his flashlight. "It's probably nothing. Bob said he left the shack unlocked so skaters could use it to get in out of the wind." A twinge of unease tugged at Liz as Jackson opened the creaky door and stepped inside, closing the door behind him.

A moment later, a ribbon of light shone beneath the door. Jackson must have turned on a lamp or lantern. Liz relaxed and practiced pirouettes with the girls.

Odd splashing sounds emanated from the shanty. Both Grace and Keturah stared at Liz, white-*Kapped* heads cocked.

What was Jackson doing?

She couldn't imagine what would delay his opening the door. Surely he would poke his head out soon.

Liz told herself that she was overreacting. But the longer he stayed in the shanty, the more her throat tightened.

Miriam skated up, her curious glance sweeping over them.

"*Mutter*, I am cold." Keturah's little mouth puckered in a pout. She shot Liz a reproachful glance. "I want to go inside the little house."

"We cannot, Keturah," Grace said in her big-sister tone. "We must wait."

"Jackson's checking to make sure no animals are inside," Liz told Miriam, "but he seems to be taking his time." She gestured with her head toward the benches and said brightly, "Maybe there's some hot chocolate left. That might keep them warm until Jackson gives the all clear."

Apparently she'd succeeded in telegraphing her uneasiness to Miriam, who said to the girls, "Let us go see."

Liz watched her cousin steer her daughters away, Keturah whining under her breath. As soon as they were out of earshot, she'd bang on the door.

Before they'd reached the benches, Jackson opened it a crack and whispered, "Are the girls still with you?"

"No, they're with Miriam. Jackson, what's the matter?"

Jackson pushed the heavy door open. He had turned on a battery-powered lamp that provided dim light. Past a gaping fishing hole in the ice, Liz saw what looked at first like a pile of wet clothes. Then she saw that they clung to an almost child-size body. Long, dark hair lay strewn around a pale face. A black Kapp sat wildly askew on her head.

"Verena Suter." Jackson spoke the name tonelessly. "I saw the top of her Kapp partially frozen in the water and pulled her out. It looks like someone struck her on the back of the head, then stuffed her into the fishing hole."

3

"Verena was murdered?" Crystal repeated, blue eyes still blank, as if Liz's words had bounced off an invisible wall between them. The skater had just made her first appearance since her afternoon arrival, only to find the Olde Mansion Inn swarming with grim-faced police and interviewees. The news apparently startled her so much that she missed an opportunity to flirt with Jackson.

The police chief, Stan Houghton, had decided to use Liz's inn for interviews rather than the police station, hoping the Amish witnesses would find it more comfortable as they described their version of the evening.

Liz had helped Houghton with past mysteries, so the chief allowed her to be present during the interrogations today. Now, sitting across from Crystal in the library, Liz held the young woman's hand, giving her time to let the horrible news sink in.

Chief Houghton, sitting beside Liz, remained silent as well. His shrewd eyes under heavy gray brows were clearly noting Crystal's silence, her slack mouth, and the horror that slowly awakened in her eyes.

"How did this happen? When?" she demanded.

"Sometime this afternoon." Chief Houghton paused. "Seems someone struck her on the head, then pushed her through an ice-fishing hole on Jaynes Lake."

"Was—was Verena still alive when—" Crystal choked on her words.

"We don't know yet. We won't know until after the autopsy."

A tear rolled down the skater's cheek. She pulled her hand from Liz's to wipe her pale face with a tissue. "I still can't believe it. She was fine when I left her."

"You and the victim were skating together, correct? At the rink on the other side of the lake?"

Crystal shook her head. "I wanted to, but Verena said we didn't have permission from the owner. She was particular about things like that." Her mouth quivered.

"Where did you skate?"

"At a little cove nearby. I don't know which direction—I get mixed up outside of Chicago."

Sighing, Houghton tapped notes into his phone. "Did anyone else know where you planned to skate? Was anyone else around?"

Crystal shrugged. "I guess Verena's family knew we were going to meet at Jaynes Lake. I told Liz and Jackson before I left, but no one else I can think of." Her forehead wrinkled. "What else did you ask me?"

"If you saw anyone else while you skated."

"Oh. Well, other skaters came and went. Crazy people on sleds zoomed down a hill onto the ice. They watched me do a few spins and clapped." A tiny smile returned to the performer's face. "But the last half hour or so, the weather got dicey and we were alone."

"Do you remember about what time that was?"

Crystal studied the ceiling. "Um, we started about one and skated for more than an hour." She turned back to the chief. "I think it was sometime between two and two thirty when I left. Yeah. Maybe about two fifteen. I knew I had plenty of extra time until my photo shoot downtown at three thirty."

"Did you go back to your room here at the inn? Or downtown?"

"No. I went for a walk around the lake."

After only an hour, you left a friend you hadn't seen in years to take a walk alone? Liz leaned forward.

Chief Houghton said nothing, but his eyebrows rose.

A slight flush colored Crystal's cheeks. "I know that sounds a little weird. Verena and I were really good friends when we were girls. She was a few years older, but we lived near each other and played together all the time. I still send her a Christmas card, since she doesn't do social media or anything. When she wrote me about getting together, I thought it would be fun. But she seemed down today."

"'Down' as in depressed? Or nervous?" The chief leaned forward.

"Some of both, I think." Crystal shrugged. "Besides, we've both changed a lot, and well, it got awkward. So I told her I had to go to the photo shoot and left early."

Yes, Liz could believe the glitzy ice star and an Amish wife and mother didn't have much in common. Perhaps Verena had been contrasting her own unhappy life with Crystal's exciting one. However, if she'd been nervous, perhaps Verena had sensed danger.

The chief said, "You were hiking the lake path, right? Did anyone see you before the photo shoot?"

Crystal nodded. "I met this really nice guy who'd come to Pleasant Creek for his work. He was trying to do his ten thousand steps for the day."

Of course, a guy. A guy with an eye out for a pretty young woman.

"What was his name? Can you describe him?" the chief asked.

"Brett Landry." She studied the ceiling. "He was maybe in his late twenties? Early thirties? Anyway, he wasn't tall, but really strong, you know? Probably works out a lot." A semblance of her gleaming smile stirred again. "Dark hair and eyes. Cute grin."

She said they'd hiked the lake path and talked so much she had been half an hour late for her photo shoot.

That must have been some conversation. Liz tried to keep her expression neutral.

The chief cleared his throat. "Did he go downtown with you?"

"No, he had a business meeting at another B&B. He'd stayed there last night."

Chief Houghton tapped on his phone. "Did he mention which bed-and-breakfast? Or his employer?"

"No. We both wanted to forget about work for a while."

Chief Houghton asked, "Do you plan on seeing Mr. Landry again?"

She brightened. "Yes, he's picking me up at nine."

"I'll still be here, so I'll need to talk to him briefly before you leave." Chief Houghton inserted a little steel into his words.

Crystal's eyes widened. "Why? Brett's such a nice guy."

"When a crime like this happens, I talk to everyone who might be helpful, no matter how unlikely. *Everyone.*"

"I guess so." Her lips puckered in a now-familiar pout. "May I go now?"

"Yes. We're done for the moment. But you're going to be in Pleasant Creek for a few days, aren't you? And for FebFest? I might need to ask you a few more questions."

"I'll be around, off and on." She sounded less than thrilled, but gave him her contact information before she left the room.

Liz, who was to bring the next interviewee into the library, followed Crystal into the rotunda. The skater paused by the door to the sitting room when Officer Jack Gerst asked for her autograph. As she complied, the skater's too-white smile and fluttering eyelids seemed far removed from her earlier grief. Did the woman lack the capacity to focus on anything besides herself? Or was she a good actress with more brains than she let on?

Throwing a smile over her shoulder, Crystal pranced up the stairs and out of sight.

In the sitting room, the Material Girls had been doing their best to help Miriam entertain Keturah, who was growing sleepy. Grace, for whom the inn was a fairy-tale world, remained content, though solemn at the evening's frightening events. For their brothers, the cookies and breads Liz had set out appeared to compensate for the long wait. Sadie told Liz that Beans, as if sensing the children's need to pet him, occasionally opened his eyes and gave them a few doggy smiles.

"He's the best dog in the world," Sadie gushed. Though Liz was Beans's official owner, Sadie considered him her canine soul mate.

Philip, who rarely came to the Olde Mansion Inn, had looked vastly uncomfortable when they all entered. Liz had intercepted the furtive glances Miriam cast at her husband, betraying growing anxiety. Like other strict Amish, Philip avoided contact with English influences as much as possible, including the police.

Over time, he had learned to trust Liz as well as Jackson. Philip and Jackson were now talking about the Borkholder farm, a conversational effort that had visibly eased his tensions—as well as Miriam's.

Liz gestured toward him, and Philip followed her into the library. As Liz had expected, he answered Houghton's questions with terse but adequate replies, describing the evening accurately. No, he had no idea who might have killed Verena Suter. Philip did not know them well, as Hiram and Verena Suter tended to keep to themselves more than most others in their community. Still, they were hardworking and did their part to help. They attended church services regularly. Yes, Philip had heard their family situation was not good, but he did not know any details.

He returned to the sitting room, and Miriam entered to answer the chief's questions. Her words echoed her husband's, except for a discreet but clear observation of the Suters—Verena and Hiram had not had a happy marriage. Verena rarely complained at women's gatherings, such as quilting bees and canning sessions, but that probably was due to the presence of her sister-in-law, Jerusha, who attended these as well. Miriam had observed that Verena and Jerusha, who lived with them, never cooperated well at these events, and Miriam imagined they experienced difficulty at home as well.

As she escorted her cousin out, Liz gave Miriam the side hug permitted by Amish relatives in public. "I'm sorry, Miriam. This was supposed to be a fun evening."

"Much harder for the Suters than for us," Miriam said, her voice betraying deep weariness. "The next days will be so difficult for them."

Along with tremendous emotional strain, the Suters would endure the scrutiny of the media—an intolerable burden for people who sought to separate themselves from the modern world.

Liz didn't want to add to the English invasion, but she hoped to show that she cared by attending Verena's funeral. Maybe she would pick up valuable tidbits about family, friends, and perhaps, even enemies—information that would help track down Verena's killer.

Liz lowered her voice. "Do you think the Suters would mind an outsider at the funeral?"

Miriam said gently, "Even if they wouldn't mind, I'm afraid the bishop would not permit an unbaptized adult to attend. But you could go with me to the viewing. That is acceptable. I will let you know when the arrangements are made."

"Thanks." Liz patted her cousin's shoulder.

Miriam nodded. "We'd better go now. Five o'clock comes early, especially with so much to do for the festival." She and Philip sold baked goods and other items from their booth.

At that moment, the front door chimes rang, and Liz opened it to find a pair of statue-still figures, an Amish man and woman, with look-alike faces so stony that their nods surprised Liz. Behind them stood Amity Bassinger, a short, plump, capable-looking woman Liz had seen helping at so many Amish events and homes, and three boys, the smallest clinging to Amity.

Officer Marlowe Dixon moved to the front of the group. "Would you tell the chief that Hiram and Jerusha Suter are here?"

Liz's heart ached for the family, especially the boys, who had pulled their black, wide-brimmed hats forward on their faces to hide their tears.

"Certainly." Liz welcomed and directed them to the sitting room. Thankfully, Miriam and Philip had not yet left, or the presence of all-English occupants might have increased the Suters' distress.

Amity helped Liz distribute cups of coffee and tea.

"You did not finish your dinner. Come, have some *Kekse*," the black-haired Amish woman coaxed the boys, offering them a plate of Liz's peanut butter cookies. "Hunger does not help sorrow."

"But I want the *Bis Zur* you brought to our house," the youngest boy protested in a teary voice. "It is the best."

Liz didn't mind that he preferred Amity's pie. The family friend was known as a champion baker.

Amity shushed him and promised he'd have a slice tomorrow. Like others of her sect, she did not show overt affection in public, even in the face of death. But her warmth seemed to help soothe their misery. She steered the youngest toward Beans, who wagged his stumpy tail.

Both Amity and Miriam appeared to comfort Verena's sons more than their aunt Jerusha, who remained beside her brother.

In a low voice, Amity said to Liz, "It is a hard thing to lose one's mother."

"Very hard." How well she knew.

"*Dänka* for your kindness."

While Miriam and her husband expressed quiet condolences, Liz returned to the library to tell Chief Houghton of the Suters' arrival.

"Bring Hiram back first," he said.

Hiram Suter followed Liz into the library, then sat awkwardly in the chair the chief indicated.

Chief Houghton leaned forward, his usually keen expression softened. "I'm so sorry for your loss, Mr. Suter."

"*Ja.*" He stared at his knees. Not a muscle moved in his lean, tanned face with its reddish-blond beard.

"Do you know of anyone who would want to harm your wife?"

"*Nay.*" The man looked Houghton directly in the face, yet seemed to avoid eye contact.

He readily answered the chief's other questions in the same low monotone. He said that Verena had hitched a ride with a neighbor to town after lunch.

Houghton said, "She went to meet her English friend, Crystal Starling, correct?"

Hiram's light-blue, almost colorless, eyes didn't blink. "Ja. A *Freund* from long ago."

Liz cautioned herself not to judge Verena's husband by his lack of emotion. The man had only learned of his wife's death within the last hour. And hadn't she herself reacted in a similar way when her mother died?

Hiram told the chief he'd sent his sons to a friend's house for the afternoon, then found Jerusha, his sister, caring for their elderly parents at their nearby *Grossdawdy Haus.* He'd informed Jerusha that he was riding to his cousin's farm, about four miles away, to see about buying a horse. However, Hiram had not found his cousin at home. He had not encountered anyone on the road either as he returned to his own farm to do chores before dinner.

Upon his arrival home, Jerusha informed him that, contrary to Verena's promise, his wife had not returned with their neighbor, who had waited an hour at their meeting place, the downtown clock tower.

Though upset, Hiram had not become alarmed until Officer Dixon had arrived.

Perhaps a storm of grief swelled inside the Amish man. But Liz noted only possible ripples—the way Hiram stuttered a little when mouthing Verena's name and the tight grasp of big, callused hands on his black-clad knees, knuckles white with effort.

Chief Houghton said gently but firmly, "I know this is very difficult for you, Hiram. But we must have an examination performed on Verena."

Slowly, her husband nodded. In a lifeless voice, he discussed picking up Verena's body afterward and taking it home for the traditional Amish viewing and funeral.

The chief said, "Your sons have suffered enough tonight. If I need to talk to them, I'll drop by your farm." After expressing his sympathy once more, the chief dismissed Hiram.

The Amish man rose, and with a wooden gait—did that betray his grief too?—returned to the sitting room. He dropped heavily onto a sofa beside two of his boys. Amity pressed a steaming cup of coffee on him, murmuring comforting words in Swiss. Mechanically, he took it but didn't drink.

Jerusha rose when Liz summoned her. Her tall, angular figure— topped by the white Kapp of the unmarried woman—strode ahead of Liz toward the library.

Houghton greeted her as she seated herself. As she had done during Hiram's interview, Liz slipped to the side and sat where she could observe Verena's sister-in-law closely without attracting too much attention to herself.

Middle-aged Jerusha possessed gray-tinged reddish-blond hair and the same angular features as her brother. She might have been attractive if deep lines hadn't eroded her forehead and mouth, and if her harsh voice didn't grate on the ear like an ungreased buggy wheel.

She confirmed that after the midday meal's cleanup, Verena had left—*deserted*, Jerusha's inflection implied. Hiram had not wanted her to go—they'd argued about her outing several days before. Verena had persisted until he gave in. However, Hiram had forbidden her to skate at "that English man's rink," though Verena's friend wanted to go there. Jerusha sniffed. "Verena must have disobeyed him anyway."

Crystal had said Verena refused to skate there, though she hadn't mentioned Hiram's mandate. What a household! Liz bit her lip, not wanting to think about the poor woman's last days there.

Jerusha went on to describe how, after Verena left, Hiram had told Jerusha he was riding to their cousin Jacob's farm. She herself had spent the afternoon caring for her elderly parents, who both suffered from dementia. When Hiram had returned, he had demanded to know where Verena was.

Jerusha's eyes narrowed. "I told him I was not his wife's keeper."

Fortunately, her neighbor Amity had stopped by, as she often did, and insisted on helping Jerusha cook the huge evening meal required for their large family.

Then, in the midst of dinner, Officer Dixon had arrived.

For the first time, a spasm of grief crossed Jerusha's face. The news of *der Mord* had broken the children's hearts. How would they get on without their Mutter?

Liz didn't dare hug the woman, but she murmured comfort as best she could.

Liz did notice, however, that Jerusha did not mention Hiram's loss. Perhaps she thought him better off without Verena?

After Liz escorted the woman back to the sitting room, the Suters and Amity left. Quickly, Chief Houghton spoke with each of the Material Girls. Apparently, he was leaving Jackson and Liz to be the last of his interviewees.

As they waited, Crystal appeared again and brewed herself a cup of coffee. She'd changed to chic silver pants with a navy tunic and stilettos, and Liz recalled that Brett Landry would soon arrive.

Chief Houghton had remembered too, as he asked Liz between interviews if Crystal's date had appeared.

Brett hadn't.

While Jackson took his turn with the chief, Liz began straightening the sitting room and refilling supplies, acting as if she didn't notice Crystal's no-show date. The skater, however, did not minimize her disgust. She flounced up to her room.

When Jackson exited the library, he noticed her absence. "The chief asked me to stay until you and he are finished, in case Landry shows up."

"Good idea, since he sent Officer Gerst out to the crime scene." Liz took two fresh mugs of coffee into the library where Chief Houghton was tapping and swiping his phone.

She handed him one, noting that his shoulders sagged ever so slightly.

"Thanks." He stretched, then took a gulp from the mug. "What a night."

"Terrible." The games of tag on the ice, the perfect skate with Jackson, and the crazy barrel-jumping contest all seemed to be from another century, not just hours before. Horror had imprinted the dead woman's face into Liz's memory forever. She shivered.

Pull yourself together.

The surviving Suters would have to deal with this murder for the rest of their lives. Recalling the boys' pain, and knowing how difficult it was to lose a mother, Liz resolved to help find whoever had killed Verena.

She said quietly, "Those poor kids. They make me think of Steve when his folks were killed."

"Your godson, right?" The chief's eyes softened. "At least he had you."

"He's grown into a fine young man." A flicker of pride lit her sadness as she thought of him serving overseas in the military. "But working through his grief took a long time."

"I'm sure." Houghton shook his head. "I wish the Amish would let themselves show more emotion. It's not fair to expect kids to keep it together when their whole world's been blown apart."

Liz hesitated, then said, "Do you think Hiram's world has been blown apart?"

"Not like theirs." The chief sipped from his mug. "Though he's shook up. No doubt about that."

"Miriam surprised me when she said outright that the Suters' marriage had problems." Liz twisted the edge of her sweater. "She'd only reveal that if it was true and she thought you needed to know it."

"She's certainly not the gossiping kind," Chief Houghton agreed, then threw Liz a wry smile. "I certainly don't think Jerusha's world has been blown apart by Verena's death."

"Not hard to see that." Had Jerusha insinuated that her sister-in-law's murder was partially her own fault? That if Verena had stayed home to help instead of gallivanting all over the county, she'd still be alive?

Or maybe Jerusha expressed her grief by spouting angry jibes she didn't mean. Liz hoped so.

The chief's voice broke in on her thoughts. "Can't imagine what it would be like to live with two women who hated each other."

"Do you think their dislike went that deep?"

Houghton gave a slight shrug. "Maybe it's too soon to say, but I sure don't see any love lost between them."

Such a sad, short life. Other than her children, no one seemed to regret Verena's death much. Not Hiram, Jerusha, or Crystal.

And none of the three, Liz realized, had alibis—unless Crystal's delinquent date showed up and supported her story. Liz told Chief Houghton about Brett Landry's absence.

He'd already noticed, of course. "He may have made up the name. Shoot, she may have made up the whole encounter with him."

At that moment, Crystal, now wearing jeans and a sequined tee, poked her head inside. "May I ask you something?"

No knock. Had she overheard the chief's conjecture?

But Crystal's face only mirrored a question. "I forgot that I'm supposed to make a guest appearance at the Fort Wayne ice rink tomorrow afternoon. No problem with that, is there?"

She appeared to be the last person who'd seen Verena alive, and Liz knew the chief preferred that she remain in Pleasant Creek.

"You'll be gone just the afternoon?" he asked.

"Overnight, actually. I'm meeting friends afterward and staying with them."

No real murder evidence gave him the right to restrict her, so Chief Houghton merely said. "All right. Please check in with me when you return."

After she nodded and ducked out, Liz ventured, "I have a question too, if you don't mind."

He gave her a tired smile. "You want permission to examine the crime scene, right?"

"You know me too well."

He harrumphed. "May as well say you can because you will. We'll be sending a couple of divers down to look for the weapon tomorrow morning. We didn't find much blood, so the perp must have stanched the blood from the head wound. So I'll have them look for a blood-stained bandage or towel too, because we didn't find that on the shore. But we should be done by afternoon."

Liz hugged herself, shivering. "That's one job I wouldn't want. Especially in the dead of winter."

"Me, either. We won't want them to stay down long. But they've got the right equipment to handle the cold. They'll be all right." His voice sharpened into a policeman's crisp directives. "Don't go alone. And report anything you think might be even a little bit relevant."

"I won't, and I will," she promised.

"Don't confuse me anymore than I already am." He rolled his

eyes and stood. "Thanks for the coffee. See you tomorrow at church, if I can shake free."

When they exited to the sitting room, where Jackson waited in case of Brett Landry's appearance, Liz noticed Crystal had stayed with him and was chattering his ear off.

She seemed oblivious when Jackson hinted that he needed to speak with Liz alone. Did he want to review details of the evening's grisly events? She couldn't imagine why, but when Crystal continued to talk, Liz gently eased Jackson out of the room to the door to her quarters.

Finally, the skater seemed to comprehend that she wasn't invited. As Liz shut her door, the annoyed *tap-tap-tap* of Crystal's stilettos echoed through the rotunda.

Jackson flopped onto Liz's sofa. "At last! I couldn't take one more minute of that woman."

"She does get a little old after a while." *Like three minutes.* Thank goodness Crystal was leaving for Fort Wayne tomorrow morning. Liz dropped beside him. "Now, what did you want to tell me?"

His wicked grin stretched from ear to ear. "Exactly what I just told you. That I couldn't stand her anymore."

Liz couldn't help chuckling, but she aimed a reproachful look at him. "I hope you don't pull this stunt very often. I'm an innkeeper, remember? I aim to attract guests, not make them mad."

"And I'm the mayor, who wants Pleasant Creek to grow and prosper." He made a face. "But I'll be just as happy if Crystal Starling doesn't bless her hometown with a visit again for a long, long time." A serious note crept into his voice. "Actually, I did want to hang out with you a little longer until I'm satisfied that you'll be safe. Someone who would bash in an unsuspecting Amish woman's head might not take kindly to a sleuth like you coming across the body."

The thought had crossed her mind. Along with the fact that the only other person staying in the inn tonight was a possible suspect. "Houghton told me he'd have Officer Dixon drive by several times tonight. But Jackson, neither you nor the police can stand guard here until they catch Verena's murderer."

"True." His wicked grin grew into a full-fledged nefarious chuckle as someone rapped on Liz's door. "However, tonight"—he gestured toward the sound—"I've lined up the next-best alternative. No, maybe better than the police."

Staring at him, Liz stood, then walked to the door and looked through her peephole.

It was Naomi.

And she was holding a small, ladylike pistol.

Liz had grown used to Sadie waving her shotgun at every opportunity. Even Mary Ann could shoot like a pro when necessary, and they'd both insisted that Liz learn.

But Naomi? Her gentle friend, who was as sweet as the pastries she baked?

"Are you going to let me in?" Naomi assumed a tough stance. "Or do I have to shoot my way in?"

"I'd let her in and let her play bodyguard tonight," Jackson advised.

"I think I will." Liz turned the dead bolt and opened the door. "When did you learn to shoot?"

"I think it was after the last time I thought we were all going to die." Naomi smiled as she entered, but the cool competence with which she slid the pistol into a holster under her arm unnerved Liz.

Liz had dealt with mysteries in the past, including a number of murders. But Naomi's new "hobby" made this one seem very, very real.

4

The next day, after church and a delightful dinner at Opal's, Liz decided to revisit the fishing shanty. Crystal had left for Fort Wayne before breakfast, so Liz had a free day.

Chief Houghton and his officers were quite thorough, so she didn't expect to find much. Still, something could have escaped their notice. Or perhaps her additional perspective might prove helpful.

"You're not going without me." Sadie, who also had dined at Opal's, relieved Naomi as Liz's bodyguard.

"And your shotgun, I suppose?" After the shock of Naomi's pistol, Liz didn't care for more firearms around.

"You betcha. With nasty weather moving in, the only people hiking around the lake are either crazy or up to no good." Sadie's blue eyes snapped. "Not to mention, a killer's running loose."

Liz soon appreciated the truth of Sadie's wisdom. Not long after they started toward the lake, roiling purple-black clouds devoured the sun, and a raw wind whipped her cheeks as they hiked along the gloomy, wooded shore. The ominous atmosphere alone made Liz appreciate her friend's cheerful presence.

If the murderer was lurking nearby—and past experience had taught Liz that killers sometimes returned to crime scenes to remove evidence or observe police action—she'd also welcome Sadie's mental fortitude and excellent marksmanship.

Surely, though, a murderer wouldn't return to the scene of his crime during broad daylight . . . though with the gathering storm, the afternoon had morphed into an uneasy dusk.

Liz flicked on her flashlight. After slipping and sliding along the slick, winding path, she and Sadie approached the area where Bob had set up the benches.

Twisting bare branches overhead warned Liz that if she wanted to uncover any evidence of the killer's movements outside, they should examine the area quickly. Rising winds might break random twigs off bushes, misdirecting their search. Additional snow would cover footprints or blood.

Blood. She remembered seeing very little in the fishing shanty. Yet when the killer slipped up behind Verena and smashed her skull, surely he couldn't have stanched the bleeding completely. The chief had been thinking something similar.

Liz motioned to Sadie. "Let's check the shanty first. I have some questions that need answers."

"Okay, Sherlock."

Liz grinned at the nickname. Much better than "Nancy Drew," which was used far too often by locals and the *Pleasant Creek News & Views* newspaper.

She pointed to a large section of water from which the ice had been removed, not far from the shanty. A thin layer of ice had re-formed over the open water below. "The chief said he was sending divers to search for the murder weapon. They must have cleared the ice here to avoid disturbing the crime scene."

"Hope they didn't weaken the ice around it. Good thing the shanty's not far from the shoreline." Sadie's eyes narrowed as she brandished the shotgun. "I'll go first."

The fishing shanty cowered over the ice as if fearing the oncoming tempest. Liz followed Sadie to the door, praying that she didn't terrify some defenseless fisherman or skater trying to keep warm. Or that her itchy finger didn't jump the gun.

Sadie positioned herself and hoisted the gun to her shoulder.

Liz knocked on the heavy, weathered door. "Hello? Anyone in there?"

Only the wind's low moan answered.

She gestured to Sadie. "I'll open it."

The door creaked as before. Liz scanned the shanty's tiny interior with her flashlight. Nothing. No one.

Sadie held the door open, turned, and faced the shore. "I'll stay here in the entry and keep an eye out for anybody who looks unfriendly. You go ahead and check it out."

As she entered, Liz first considered the noisy old door whose sound had caught her ear. Between the size of the place and that audible warning, no one could have entered the hut without an occupant knowing it.

She turned on the hut's battery-powered light and saw the tattered camp chair on the opposite side of the fishing hole, facing it. A couple of benches had been built into the wall. A grungy cabinet held a sparse collection of fishing supplies and an old insulated bottle.

She took a second look at the hole, now frozen over. In the trauma of finding Verena, Liz hadn't noticed that the fishing hole was unusually large.

Of course. Otherwise, how could someone have shoved a body into it?

Liz knelt with her flashlight. The hole appeared to be an odd-shaped fusion of several holes. The perpetrator probably had used a hand auger, as a power auger's noise would have drawn attention. The hole's edges looked smooth, not broken. Either a fisherman had anticipated catching shark-sized fish, or the killer had widened the hole—perhaps in preparation for hiding the body? Liz shivered again.

She turned her attention back to the noisy door. Crystal said Verena had avoided Bob's rink. Given that mindset, she probably wouldn't have chosen to warm up or change into skates in the shanty either.

Besides, if Verena were removing her skates inside when the murderer entered, the sound quickly would have warned her of his presence. And if Verena had sat in the camp chair to remove her skates, how had the killer managed to strike her on the back of the head? He would have had to wedge himself into the almost nonexistent space behind the chair before she arrived, and she would have had to miss seeing him when she came in the door, which, given the size of the shanty, would have been basically impossible. If she'd sat on one of the benches on either side, he would have had to strike her in the face, not the back of her head.

It seemed likely Verena had met her death elsewhere.

Perhaps the chair had faced away from the doorway, and Jackson had moved it when he pulled the body out of the fishing hole. Liz tried to recall any signs that the woman had fought her attacker, such as bruises or scrapes on hands or face. There were none that she remembered, so it was likely that she had either known her attacker or had been unaware of his presence.

Liz kneeled and, using the flashlight, searched every inch of the icy floor, then scrutinized the walls. She hadn't recalled seeing blood there when they found Verena. Now Liz discovered only a few drops here and there—not what she would have expected from such an extensive head wound. Had the killer risked taking time to clean up such evidence? Would he have done so when fishermen, skaters, or clubhouse-seeking kids were likely to interrupt?

No, given Liz's earlier doubts and the chance of surprise visitors, the scales still seemed tipped toward Verena having been murdered elsewhere.

Sadie, still facing toward the outside, asked, "Is anything making sense yet?"

"Maybe." Liz's questions about the lack of blood had given birth to new ones. If Verena had been murdered elsewhere, why had the murderer brought her here? Unless she'd been killed nearby and the hut presented the best hiding place.

Liz quickly summarized what she'd found. "The chief didn't say where he thought Verena died. I'm thinking she was killed elsewhere and moved here. Crystal said they were skating a short distance away from the benches in a little cove that protected them from the wind. Let's take a look around."

No sleet or snow had fallen yet, though the sky had darkened even more. Liz's flashlight guided them as they walked toward the area east of Bob's benches.

Sadie, clasping her gun, peered suspiciously from side to side like a sheriff in an old cowboy movie.

Dear Sadie. Sadie sometimes drove her friends insane, but they never doubted her all-or-nothing loyalty. Even in this sad context, she made Liz smile. And Sadie was right, Liz reminded herself. This was no ordinary stroll along the lake. She needed to stay on her guard.

Prominent *No Trespassing* signs posted along the shore stopped them in their tracks.

"I can't imagine Verena would ignore those and skate here," Liz said.

"Nope. Wouldn't be her style," Sadie agreed.

They hiked in the opposite direction. They hadn't walked far past the shanty when the shoreline receded almost to the path.

"This might be their cove." Liz surveyed their surroundings. "Just enough of a dip to shelter them from the wind. Close to the ice so they wouldn't have to walk far on skates."

"I'll bet somebody's been sledding here, anyway," Sadie observed.

"How can you tell?" Liz swung her flashlight, looking for tracks on the ice.

Sadie pointed behind them. "They used that rotten log over there. We used to do that when we were kids and didn't have enough sleds for everyone. We'd find an old log and turn it into a sled."

Liz aimed the flashlight at it. "Somebody sawed one end."

"It's easy to do when the wood is soft. Those 'sleds' go surprisingly fast on the ice."

The fun memory eased their macabre search, but only for a moment. Liz hoped all the sledding hadn't accidentally destroyed important evidence.

Liz realized that they couldn't see the shanty from this point. "Still, if you knew where the shanty was, it would be the perfect place to hide a body. Not enough woods around here to conceal one well, and drilling a large enough hole in the open ice, then stuffing a body in—well, someone would probably notice. Better to park a car by the road. It's also close by, with no houses along that stretch." Liz gestured. "Then stuff the body into the trunk, park near on the shore as close to the shanty as possible, and sneak it inside. I wonder if any witnesses saw a car there or just happened to see the murderer in action." With the lake being such a public site, the chief might find it difficult to track anyone down.

Sadie prodded, "Crystal seems to have been the last person who saw Verena alive. I know Chief Houghton likes to keep his hunches quiet, but has anybody come up with a reason she might want to kill Verena?"

"Not that I know of." Though the chief certainly didn't tell Liz all he knew or suspected.

Liz imagined Hiram or Jerusha Suter using a wagon or buggy to transport Verena's body. Leaving horses alone beside a road seemed risky, as any number of causes might spook the animals, and she didn't see a good place to tie them up. Whoever it was would have needed a partner.

Liz gulped. Could Hiram and his sister have conspired to get rid of Verena? Only Hiram could confirm Jerusha's whereabouts that afternoon—their parents, suffering from dementia, couldn't be considered reliable observers. Jerusha had supported Hiram's claim that he'd gone to his cousin's, but since no one had seen him, no other witnesses could verify that.

Using her flashlight again, Liz walked along the cove's shore, eyeing a swath of the rocky earth and patches of snow. Sadie stood like a sentinel, head slowly swiveling as she surveyed the surrounding expanse of fallen trees. The lake had flooded sometime over the past year, taking its toll on some of the shoreline vegetation and scanty trees and bushes.

She continued to sweep her gaze back and forth. Behind another log, she found what she sought: a patch of black mud, disturbed by some sort of tool. A hand hoe? A sharp stick?

On the log itself were several rusty-looking patches—Verena's blood, most likely. The mud behind the log probably had absorbed the majority of the flow from her injury.

"Are you all right?" Sadie paused in her vigilance to look Liz's way.

"Not really." Her stomach twisted as she thought of Verena removing her skates, perhaps considering an hour's getaway downtown before returning to her sad life on the farm.

Still clutching her gun, Sadie walked over and rubbed Liz's shoulder.

Liz told her friend what she'd found. "I'm almost positive this is where Verena died." She gestured at the log. "Those bushes on either side would have blocked the view from anyone walking along the path and would've partially impeded a skater's view." Liz gritted her teeth, eyes moistening. "It's not a perfect place to murder someone, but it would do."

For a moment, Sadie said nothing, an indication of her own sorrow. Then, "You think the chief knows about this?"

"I'm sure he does." Numerous footprints in the old snow and moist earth confirmed her gut feeling. "But I won't disturb anything until I've talked to him." Liz pulled out her phone and called.

The chief, who had just risen from a Sunday nap, confirmed that he and his officers had tracked down the murder site. "We've taken pictures and samples for testing, of course, but I'm sure that's where the poor woman was killed. Find anything else?"

"Probably not." She described her and Sadie's observations at the shanty.

The chief mostly grunted in response, but when Liz asked if he or the officers had widened the hole during their investigation, he said, "Why would we do that?"

His tone told her she'd asked enough questions for one Sunday afternoon.

Besides, her uncertainties regarding the lack of blood and the chair's position had been answered by her discovery of the real crime scene. After she hung up, she and Sadie tramped the stretch of land up to the road. They found plenty of footprints—probably those of the police—and a few broken twigs. But no blood or evidence turned up that the body had been dragged, reinforcing Liz's suspicion that the murder had involved more than one person.

As if to emphasize the storm of possibilities, the blackening sky unleashed a barrage of sleet that sent Liz and Sadie stumbling back to the inn.

"Boy, you sure know how to spend a peaceful Sunday afternoon," Sadie quipped as they burst through the back door, covered with ice.

Warm peach pie à la mode with mugs of hot coffee seemed an absolute necessity. Even Sadie, usually too restless to read much, settled happily with Liz before the sitting room's crackling fire with a Louis L'Amour novel. That evening, making homemade caramel corn and watching a funny movie made bedtime a less daunting prospect.

Later, though, as tortured tree skeletons rattled bony fingers at Liz's dark bedroom window, she lay wide awake. Attempts to push horrific murder scenes from her mind appeared futile.

Maybe a little warm milk might induce sleep.

However, Sadie snored on Liz's sofa bed, loaded shotgun at her side.

Did she even dare risk a trip to the bathroom tonight?

There were more scratching noises at her windows. This storm had encouraged the inn, more than a hundred years old, to display its scariest collection of unknown thumps and creaks. She heard a crunch outside. A footstep?

Liz froze, mid-breath. Had she heard another?

No, probably debris that had tumbled to the ice-covered ground. Even so, she wished that Beans had chosen to sleep in her quarters rather than in the foyer.

A huge *thump* outside sent her and the bedclothes halfway to the ceiling.

Before Liz landed, Sadie was there and pointing the shotgun at the window. "Whazzat?" She drew the shade and peered outside. "Can't see a darn thing. Why don't you have your lights on?"

"I do—around the rest of the inn. If I turn this one on, it keeps me awake."

"Branch fell off the big maple," Sadie muttered. "Doesn't look like it hit anything."

Liz's first interpretation of the "footsteps" probably was accurate. Small limbs had crunched into the snow before the whole branch had gone down. Nothing more.

Within minutes, Sadie was snoring again, and Liz's eyelids drooped, a promising sign of blessed slumber. Before they could close, a shred of light flashed in the window.

Headlights? But her windows faced no roads or driveways. And no one in his right mind would be fishing, skating, or hiking around the lake on a night like this.

Her eyelids froze open once again. Someone was definitely outside.

5

"**B**eans, couldn't you sleep a little longer? Just half an hour?" A sleep-deprived Liz, dragging herself to the inn's foyer, stretched her jaws in a yawn. "You'll probably snore away ninety percent of the day. I can't."

The bulldog stared at her, unblinking and unwavering in his demands.

Sadie, Beans's number-one fan, still snuggled under her quilts on Liz's nice, soft sofa.

"If she adores you so much, why doesn't she let you out?" Liz muttered as she flipped on the porch light, yanked the front door open, and watched as he ambled around the corner of the inn.

For a moment, she allowed herself to revel in the wintry landscape and her gingerbread-trimmed porch, where fresh snow looked like a dusting of sugar. The downtown clock tower sweetly chimed optimism that morning would indeed dawn.

Strange how the storm's fury could coat the world with spectacular white beauty—beauty that would have to be shoveled. She often hired handymen to do the big jobs. Since she was wide awake, though, and the new snowfall wasn't deep, she might as well shovel it herself. Liz threw on a parka and boots. She cleaned off the front porch and sidewalk, then tramped to the back steps to shovel them as well.

A small magenta box shone against the white snow. Because of the color, she immediately thought of Crystal. Had Brett Landry shown up late and left an apology when he saw no lights inside the inn?

Maybe she'd heard Brett's footsteps last night. But why wouldn't he have come to the front door?

Liz picked up the waterproofed wicker box. A smart choice of packaging and very attractive. Had she noticed similar boxes at Sweet Everything? She couldn't recall any. The small envelope taped to a silver bow on top bore Liz's name.

Not much inspired a huge smile at seven in the morning, but this gift accomplished it. She held the parchment card up to light streaming from the kitchen windows and read its elegant calligraphy: *Be my valentine.*

Jackson. He must be looking forward to the Sweetheart Dance as much as she. She slid the top off the box.

Even in the shadowy light, she knew she'd never seen a more beautiful cupcake. Swirls of white frosting graced it, topped with a lattice heart decorated with tiny pink roses. A ruby dot at the base of the heart hinted of raspberry or cherry filling.

After such a restless night, this was a lovely beginning to the day. Could she bring herself to eat such a work of art?

Absolutely. Maybe for breakfast. First, though, she'd take pictures and send them to the other Material Girls. And sometime today, she'd thank Jackson and tell him she couldn't wait until the dance.

Liz didn't realized Beans was still there until he uttered a reproachful harrumph.

"Sorry, boy. How long have you been waiting?" Carefully, she closed the box, hugged it to her, and let Beans inside. She debated the setting for the photo. Did she want the polished wood of the big, old-fashioned dining room table as the background? Or should she have the cupcake beside the antique crystal vase of roses on the sitting room mantel? She opted for the vase, situated the cupcake, and aimed her phone.

Perfect.

This was so different from other unpleasant surprises she'd received on her porch. Liz made a face. Not long ago, one intimidator had left a deer skull. Liz shuddered and focused again on the cupcake.

Mmm. One finger reached for just a taste of the frosting. And halted.

What if Jackson hadn't sneaked this onto her porch last night?

Who else in Pleasant Creek would have braved that storm? Sadie's and Jackson's concerns about her safety echoed through her head. As she gazed at the exquisite treat, a chill spiraled up her back.

Don't be so paranoid, she scolded herself. Jackson had probably left the cupcake. But later this morning, she'd double-check, just to make sure.

"Until then, you stay in your box in the pantry." She'd busy herself elsewhere so she wouldn't be tempted to eat it before she confirmed where it had come from.

With Crystal gone until later that day and Sadie planning to sleep until nine, Liz didn't have to cook breakfast right now. Nevertheless, she made herself an omelet to fuel her morning—and keep her mind off the cupcake. With a houseful of guests coming for FebFest at the end of the week, she didn't lack tasks to occupy her. Sarah had asked for the day off, so laundry and deep-cleaning bathrooms more than filled the next couple of hours.

By then, the possibility that her imagination had run wild wilted her resolve. "What will I say if I do call Jackson?" she asked Beans. "Did you leave a gorgeous valentine cupcake on my doorstep last night? Or is some other guy madly in love with me?"

Beans didn't so much as twitch. Her quandary obviously didn't register the tiniest blip on his radar.

"You don't really think Verena's killer would try to poison me, do you?" His jowl-shaking snore reassured her.

"Poison you?!" Sadie's shriek didn't do much for Beans's morning beauty sleep either. Grumbling under his breath, he waddled off to the four-season room.

Halfway through Liz's explanation to Sadie, Mary Ann arrived to open Sew Welcome, and Liz had to repeat her concerns about the cupcake.

Mary Ann's mouth tightened. "If you don't call Jackson, I will."

"No, no, I'll call Naomi first." Why hadn't she thought of this before? Liz hit her speed dial.

Her friend answered, sounding out of breath. "Sorry, I can't chat. Business is good this morning."

"I'll make it quick," Liz promised and told Naomi about the cupcake, omitting her fears about it.

"I baked similar cupcakes for a New Year's wedding," Naomi said, "but nothing recently. Maybe Jackson wanted to keep it hush-hush and bought it from a Marion bakery. Or maybe your secret admirer is from out of town." She teased, "Perhaps that hunky Chris Blaine?"

At the mention of a former guest who had tried to romance her, Liz frowned. "No, he canceled his business retreat, remember? After I told him we had no future."

"Just a minute, sir," Naomi called to a customer.

"I'll let you go now so you can get back to work."

"I'm sorry I couldn't be more help." Naomi ended the call.

Mary Ann cocked her head. "So Naomi didn't bake it?"

"No." Liz hit speed dial again before she changed her mind. "I may as well call Jackson."

Jackson answered on the first ring. "I was just going to call you." His warm voice held a note of concern as he continued, "Any problems last night?"

"Um, well, I'm not sure."

His voice sharpened. "What do you mean, you're not sure?"

Stumbling a little, she told him.

Silence on the other end. Then, "No, I didn't leave it on your porch. I wish I had. But that's beside the point—with this murderer on the loose, you shouldn't accept anything without being sure of its origin, no matter how harmless it looks."

Of course. Given the circumstances, Jackson never would have left an anonymous gift for her. "I'll tell the chief about the cupcake. Maybe he'll want to have it analyzed."

"He certainly will." Jackson sounded almost irritable. "Is Sadie still there?"

"Yeah, and Mary Ann made it in through the snow too."

"Good. Because this worries me." His voice grew stern. "No alone time today, okay? And please call the chief now. Or I will."

"I'll call him." She had almost too many good friends.

When Liz informed Chief Houghton of her "gift," he agreed, though his voice barely cloaked a small chuckle when Liz mentioned Jackson. "The mayor probably doesn't like the idea of some other guy leaving you a present. But I think he's right. Hate to mess up your pretty cupcake, but we need to know what it's made of."

Sighing, Liz told him she'd bring it to the station soon.

"Thank goodness," Mary Ann hugged Liz, then strode to Sew Welcome's door and inserted her key.

Sadie patted her arm. "I'll get my own breakfast this morning and fix us coffee. *You* just stay safe."

And she was supposed to do that how? Certainly not by spending the day shut up in a closet. First, she'd take the cupcake to the police station, then stock up on groceries before FebFest. Then maybe she'd stop by Naomi's on the way back and devour one of her incredible cream-filled, definitely not toxic key lime cupcakes as consolation. Then she'd take care of business at the inn until Crystal arrived.

As she carried out her plan, she almost forgot the turmoil of the weekend. The satisfaction of a full pantry organized, spreadsheets completed, and baseboards dusted soothed her mind.

In the quiet afternoon hours, Liz scanned online articles about Crystal. She certainly didn't expect that she'd uncover hostilities between the skater and any Amish, but one never knew.

Her gut was proven right in this instance. Nothing she read presented any conceivable reason Crystal would attack her childhood friend.

Liz also perused the sale of quilts online, hoping to find some trace of the stolen ones. She didn't expect the thief to post them on any online auction sites, but she checked anyway, then browsed several quilting sites. Liz hadn't realized how many quilts included patchwork stars, and she lost track of how many white wedding-ring quilts she found. Mary Ann and Sadie had described unique features of the Klassy and Oertl quilts, but such details often didn't show up in pictures online.

When all the quilts began to look alike, she decided it was time to shift gears and prepare for coffee hour.

Liz baked a dozen sugar cookies, but refrained from her usual sample, as yesterday's treats and the key lime cupcake that morning had blown her treat-calorie allowance for a month. She hoped Crystal would arrive soon and eat some of the cookies. If not, she'd take them to Sew Welcome and push them on Sadie and Mary Ann, neither of whom seemed to have gained a pound since 1975.

Liz needn't have worried because Jackson showed up, hungry and chatty. He also presented her with a single red rose.

So you didn't like being upstaged by a murderer, huh? Liz thought with good humor as the flower's fragrance wafted past her nose. "Thank you," she said out loud. The guy beside her on the sitting room sofa really was the most considerate, caring man she'd ever met.

"You're very, very welcome." Jackson melted her with his smile. Then he devoured four cookies within a few minutes while she set about putting the rose in a bud vase.

Conversation revolved around the murder and Jackson's concern for her safety. But she managed to steer their chat toward FebFest, hoping they might stumble on the subject of the Sweetheart Dance.

Instead, Jackson bemoaned his struggles with Daryl French, a vendor who continued to harass him about reserving several booths at the event.

"This guy is a real piece of work." Jackson shook his head. "I've heard reports from other mayors and festival coordinators about French's passing off cheap substitutes as genuine Amish articles, especially quilts. I've tried to brush him off with my usual awesome diplomacy—"

"I'll bet your modesty impressed him too." Liz grinned.

"I guess I made no impression at all, because he keeps bugging me." Jackson exhaled. "So this morning, I wrote him an official letter. I also called him and told him outright that he was banned not only from FebFest, but from any other events in Pleasant Creek."

"I'm sure that made his day."

"Probably not." Jackson winced. "I hope he doesn't sue the town. Or me."

"Don't let French get you down. You have to be strong for FebFest." Liz lowered her voice. "Don't tell Sadie, but I've already laid a bet that you'll beat her at the Frozen Turkey Bowl."

"Really?"

At his astonished expression, she giggled. "No. But I hope you're looking forward to the festival." She touched the rose he'd given her. "I know I am."

Jackson's eyes softened, and he took her hand. "You're so right. I need to think about what's important."

"Jackson!" Crystal's blinding smile spotlighted him. "I didn't know you'd be here."

She sashayed past Liz and stooped, throwing her arms around him.

With Crystal's sequined body blocking her view, Liz couldn't see Jackson's expression. She imagined it resembled that of the raccoon she'd once trapped with a laundry basket.

"Welcome back, Crystal," Liz said sweetly. "Have some cookies."

"Oh, no." She straightened. "Can't be a figure skater if you don't keep your figure, you know."

Liz detected Jackson's attempt to hide his eye roll. She grinned.

The skater chattered endlessly about her appearances, her fans, and her big plans.

As an innkeeper, Liz had grown accustomed to all kinds of guests, including those less than pleasant to serve. She accepted them as part of her business and also as part of her calling. But if he was so annoyed, why didn't Jackson leave, for goodness' sake?

Then slowly, understanding dawned. He'd made up his mind to stay and protect Liz. However, Crystal apparently had made up her mind she would stay as well.

Despite Jackson's "usual awesome diplomacy," Crystal didn't appear to understand his hints and invited herself to dinner. She accompanied them to Mama's Home Cooking, where she ended up signing numerous autographs and all but taking a bow.

When she also tried to invite herself to Liz's quarters, Jackson abandoned any semblance of subtlety as he barricaded the door. "Liz has been through a lot the past couple of days and needs quiet this evening," he told Crystal. "I'm sure you understand." His artificial smile gleamed almost as much as the skater's.

Liz thought Crystal would suggest he depart as well. Instead, she shrugged. "I suppose that happens when you get older." She shot Liz a similar faux smile and flounced toward the stairs.

Crystal hadn't yet pushed the limit of Liz's patience. But almost.

"Sure you want to hang out in the geriatric wing?" she teased Jackson.

He snorted. "You're anything but a little old lady, Liz."

They watched a fun movie, and Liz forgot he was protecting her until its ending.

As they walked to her door, Jackson grimaced. "I hate to think the only person here with you tonight is Crystal."

"I'll be fine. The chief promised an officer would patrol the inn regularly until we learn if that cupcake was doctored."

Oops. She shouldn't have mentioned the cupcake, because Jackson's frown now wrinkled his forehead.

"If we didn't live in a small town, I'd crash on your sitting room sofa until this murder is solved," he informed her.

The thought of his nearness sounded very nice. "And risk an encounter with Crystal?"

He snorted again. "Encounter? More like an ambush. Would you walk me to the front door? If she *is* lurking out there, I might say something really mean. Or do something desperate."

Liz hid a grin as he peeked out the door and scanned the rotunda and stairway.

"All quiet?" she whispered.

"Appears so." He still glanced from side to side as she accompanied him to the front entrance. "Text me when you're safely locked inside your quarters, okay?"

Liz nodded, then watched him tramp through the snow down the street.

She really had appreciated his determination to keep her safe tonight.

However—she felt a wicked smirk creep across her face—when it came right down to it, who had been protecting whom?

6

The next morning, Liz figured that Verena's autopsy should have been completed. But that didn't mean Chief Houghton would share the results with her.

Having coaxed a slightly pouty Crystal into eating a large, fattening breakfast, Liz spent her cleanup time trying to deduce how she would obtain those facts. Dr. Sam Schneider, Pleasant Creek's physician and coroner, certainly wouldn't disclose them without the family's written consent. And even if Hiram Suter—suspect or not—would be willing to share them, she would not trouble him or his family when they hadn't yet buried Verena.

Pleasant Creek News & Views probably would publish the official cause of death in its weekly Friday edition. But a trail could grow quite cold in a few days. A murderer could disappear forever. Recalling the numb grief of Verena's boys, Liz scrubbed frying pans with a vengeance.

A face popped into her thoughts. Rob Carver—the red-haired, freckled senior reporter for the newspaper. Rob surely would write the story for *News & Views*. He'd probably already wheedled Verena's autopsy report from somewhere.

When she called the paper, Rob was out, so she had to leave a message. But he returned her call before she'd finished cleaning Crystal's messy room.

"What's up, Liz?" Rob's breezy, friendly manner probably made most people let down their guard, but she knew better.

She matched his positive tone. "I read your account of Verena

Suter's death—quite accurate and to the point. Since I was there, I doubly appreciated the fact it wasn't exaggerated or lurid."

"Thanks." He sounded gratified, but a little wary. "Not everyone understands the challenge of reporting the news."

She pressed, "I imagine you've probably discovered more about the case since then. Could you tell me anything about Verena's autopsy results?"

For a second, Rob remained silent. Then, "I'd be glad to exchange information with you, Liz, if that's what you're asking. I assume that you're working on the Suter case—"

"Not officially," she said hastily. Houghton wouldn't like a front-page article about her role in attempting to find the killer.

"I've heard plenty about your 'unofficial' cases." She heard a grin in his voice. "We probably could help each other out. If I tell you what I know, then I'd appreciate being the first to know about any progress you make in finding the killer."

"You would be the first reporter I'd tell," Liz agreed.

"Fair enough." Rob said, "The autopsy report stated that Verena Suter was knocked unconscious with a heavy object—possibly a hammer—then drowned when her attacker hid her under the ice."

Liz suppressed a shudder. "A hammer could be from anywhere. There must be a million toolboxes in this county. Did the coroner note any indication that she fought her attacker?"

"No. The injuries suggest that he sneaked up behind her. Mrs. Suter probably didn't know what hit her." Now Rob probed a little: "Say, have you or the police come up with a motive as to why someone would want to kill the poor woman?"

"Not yet." She wouldn't reveal any suspicions until she unearthed solid evidence. "Have you heard anything about fingerprints, DNA results, or other lab tests?"

"Doc said the police found no fingerprints on the body. Not

surprising, since it's definitely glove weather and she was drowned." He sniffed. "Houghton pretty much put a clamp on the rest of that info."

She'd expected as much. "I'm grateful for your help, Rob."

"And I'll look forward to yours." He hung up.

Liz hadn't learned much from the phone call, but at least had confirmed what had seemed obvious. Though she knew he could be a pest when following a story, an alliance with Rob might prove productive.

Liz pushed away thoughts about Verena's murder, anticipating the first of her FebFest guests, Toni McIntyre, who would arrive this afternoon. While Sarah cleaned and polished, Liz baked goodies and decorated the inn for the festival.

She'd expected an influx of couples so close to Valentine's Day. However, her reservation list included a women's group who would occupy the rest of the second-floor rooms and two male snowmobile enthusiasts who had reserved the Sunrise and Sunset Rooms on the third floor.

Hearts and cupids might not fit this bunch, so Liz decided to minimize their use. But she did arrange a cheerful little bouquet of red carnations and yellow and white daisies—her first purchase from Heaven-Scent Flowers, the new florist in town—in a crockery pitcher and placed it in the Amish Room where Toni and her roommate, Sofia Lopez, would stay. Before the main group arrived, Liz would scatter similar arrangements in the other rooms and among the antiques she displayed in hallways and on stairway landings.

This moment, though, she paused to drink in the beauty of Amish-crafted furniture and the warmth of the patchwork quilt, bright-hued pillows, and rag rugs—all far more colorful than the local Amish bishop allowed. He didn't even allow cushions on chairs. But the overall effect retained the simplicity of Amish design, and guests loved the room's homey ambiance.

Toni arrived, as expected, early in the afternoon. Though middle-aged, she reminded Liz of a breathless little girl, late to class. Her round, faded-denim eyes held more than a hint of fear.

"Is something wrong?" Liz fought the urge to slip an arm around Toni's plump shoulders.

"I was listening to the radio as I drove into Pleasant Creek." She gestured toward the back of the inn. "Is it true somebody drowned an Amish woman in your lake?"

Oh, no. The nervous type. Though Liz had to admit this case made her nervous too. She answered, "The Olde Mansion Inn only borders Jaynes Lake—I don't own it. But yes, I'm sorry to say that report is true. Still, we have an excellent police department that will not quit until that person is brought to justice."

Toni twisted a lock of lank, light-brown hair. "Oh, dear. Of course, I had no idea of that when I made reservations."

None of us did. The devastated faces of Verena's boys flashed through Liz's mind.

She steered her thoughts back to Toni's worries. "The police chief and his officers patrol this area every night."

"That—that's good to know. But I'd better check with the others to see if they still want to come." She pulled out her phone.

Liz took several slow breaths to calm her galloping heart. The loss of income on three rooms times four nights would demolish her February budget. If this group canceled, could she count on last-minute FebFest attendees to fill in some of the blanks on her spreadsheets?

"Would you like a cup of coffee while you decide?" she asked quietly.

"Yes, yes, that would be nice." Toni's chubby face drooped. "I'm so sorry to disturb things. I hate to upset people. But they put me in charge of reservations, you see, and—hello, Bunny? I'm here at the Olde Mansion Inn. Yes, yes, it's lovely, but I found out today they've had a murder practically in the backyard. I'm so sorry. I didn't want to do anything you girls wouldn't like."

Before Toni could apologize again for a murder she didn't commit, Liz hurried to the sitting room coffee machine. When she brought a mugful to the distraught woman, Toni had just hung up.

Inhaling the brew's steamy fragrance seemed to settle her nervous guest a little. With her hands wrapped around the mug's comforting warmth, Toni told Liz, "Bunny's checking with the rest of the Sisterhood."

Sisterhood? Nuns, maybe? Though Liz had never heard of a nun named Bunny. "Would you like to sit until you hear from them?"

"That would be wonderful." On the way to the sitting room, Toni glanced around the rotunda and stairway. Her gaze halted at Sew Welcome. "Oh, there's the quilting shop I saw online. Actually, that's why I chose this B&B. Your rooms looked very nice, of course, but I love quilts and quilting."

"I can introduce you to the owners, Mary Ann Berne and Sadie Schwarzentruber, if you'd like." She led Toni through the shop's door.

Its bell jingled a friendly greeting that matched Mary Ann's. "Is this your new guest? So glad you dropped in!"

Soon they were chatting about quilting like old friends. Sadie joined the conversation, and Toni smiled for the first time. Her smile widened when Bunny of the Sisterhood called back and confirmed that the group would arrive the next day as planned, and stay at the Olde Mansion Inn for FebFest.

After Toni hung up, Sadie invited her to the Material Girls' quilting session that night. "We'd love to have you. We have so much fun, and Naomi always brings some kind of treat. She dropped a hint that she was bringing her sweet rolls tonight." Sadie licked her lips.

"Her sweet rolls are famous all over the state," Liz agreed. "They should be *world* famous."

"You really must join us, Toni," Mary Ann urged, flashing her irresistible smile.

"I—well, I suppose I could."

The invitation and the sight of the Amish Room when Liz showed it to her brought a faint flush of color to her cheeks. "How lovely! Photos just couldn't do it justice."

Liz left Toni happily unpacking and returned to her rotunda desk to do paperwork.

Later Toni descended, dressed to brave the wintry afternoon. "I need to confirm some details about our group's booth with the town hall."

The animation she'd displayed while talking with Sadie and Mary Ann had drained away. Did she anticipate problems with Jackson's office? Or perhaps an unfamiliar town, though small, presented too big a challenge for Toni.

Liz offered, "I need to go downtown sometime this afternoon too. Would you like me to accompany you?"

"No thank you. I'll use the GPS on my phone." Toni hurried toward the foyer door.

Liz had just pulled out her own phone to confirm a reservation when a scream erupted from the foyer.

"He's dead!"

Confusion reigned for a split second in Liz's mind until she realized what must have happened. She hurried to reassure Toni that Beans indeed possessed a heartbeat.

Toni's hand went to her own heart. "When I tripped over him, he didn't stir. I thought maybe I'd killed him—"

"No, no, Beans is just fine." Liz poked one of the bulldog's legs in a ticklish spot that generated an indignant flick of his ear. "See?"

After Toni left, finally convinced she hadn't killed Beans, Liz considered two recover-from-Toni strategies—she could either take a short nap or drink an extra-strong, giant cup of coffee.

She opted for coffee in the four-season room. The room's large windows featured a gorgeous view of icy Jaynes Lake and its sparkling, snowy surroundings. Liz let her head and shoulders relax on the sofa's cushiony back while the afternoon sun warmed her bones.

Thank goodness Crystal was practicing, then making another appearance in Marion today, so Liz could enjoy a moment of solitude. The skater wasn't due back until coffee hour. Would Toni come to coffee hour too? Liz had forgotten to ask. Toni and Crystal—that would be quite a mix.

Perhaps when Toni's group arrived tomorrow, the woman would relax a bit more. Though it seemed that every time Toni did or said something connected with this Sisterhood, she shriveled. Maybe she was brand-new at handling group responsibilities. Or maybe Toni just needed an evening of quilting and fun with the Material Girls. Remembering the woman's smiles at Sew Welcome, Liz also relaxed—too much.

She startled awake. How long had she been snoozing? She still needed to pick up a few more items for the weekend!

Her phone assured her she'd been asleep only half an hour. The nap had refreshed Liz, and a brisk walk downtown before coffee hour would energize her for a busy evening.

She mailed a few business letters, then headed for the grocery store a couple of blocks off the town square.

Not every town has hitching posts for buggies. Though she'd become accustomed to Pleasant Creek's unique links with the Amish community, such features still fascinated Liz, who had grown up in Boston. Whereas some towns appeared dreary during winter, the Swiss chalet style of most of the downtown buildings gave Pleasant Creek an Alpine air—without the mountains, of course. The occasional buggy added to the foreign effect. Brilliant banners advertising FebFest hung from every vintage streetlight.

Approaching the grocery's parking lot, Liz came upon a curious sight. Toni was standing by a buggy, talking to Jerusha. Liz stepped behind the trunk of a big maple tree to watch the exchange, which seemed to consist of more than, "What's the right way back to the Olde Mansion Inn?" Toni and her friends were from Coldwater, Michigan. How did she know Jerusha?

And why am I hiding behind a tree? Liz was glad she didn't have to explain this to anyone because she couldn't explain it to herself.

After a few minutes, the conversation ended. Jerusha climbed into her buggy and drove off without a backward glance, as if they had just conducted a business transaction. Toni, however, wrung her hands and hurried away. Was she returning to the town square, or perhaps to the inn?

Liz attempted to cross her path, but the woman, without warning, wheeled and headed down a side street. When Liz reached it, Toni had disappeared. Liz searched a couple of blocks, but her guest seemed to have vanished. How did she move so quickly through the snow? More importantly, why?

Surely she had seen and recognized Liz. Why would Toni avoid her?

Liz tried to recall something she'd said or done wrong—then shrugged. Perhaps whatever was bothering the woman consumed her so completely that she'd seen nothing but her trouble.

But what would Jerusha have to do with Toni's trouble? Questions slipped and slid through Liz's mind like unsteady skaters. However, her phone beeped, reminding her that coffee hour was in an hour, so she'd better make her purchases and hurry back to the inn.

She returned with ten minutes to spare. Liz almost expected her newest guest to continue to avoid her, especially as her car was gone. There was no sign of Crystal's flashy SUV in the parking lot either.

Why was she obsessing over coffee hour when probably no one

would show up? Still pondering Toni's conversation with Jerusha, Liz slapped half a dozen just-in-case balls of snickerdoodle dough onto a sheet and shoved the tray into the oven. She'd dusted the sitting room earlier. She hadn't had time to vacuum, but only a handful of crumbs sprinkled the dark carpet. She didn't bother with the paper lace doilies and fanned napkins she often used.

Liz brought a tray containing the small cream pitcher, sugar bowl, cinnamon tin, coffee flavorings, and teas into the sitting room.

Because she'd already consumed sufficient caffeine for the day, she brewed herself a mug of decaf, mostly to fill the room with a welcoming fragrance. Dropping onto the settee, she replayed all the details of Verena's murder through her mind. She brainstormed their implications, hoping she and Chief Houghton hadn't missed something important.

The chime of the front doorbell startled her, causing her to splash coffee on her khakis. Scrubbing the spots with a napkin as she walked, Liz answered the door. Jackson stood on the step, which wasn't unusual, as he occasionally dropped in for coffee hour. But he never rang the doorbell. An odd smile strained his face.

A woman stood beside him—a tall, svelte woman with Jackson's thick, tawny hair and hazel eyes, but minus his twinkle.

Jackson coughed. "Liz, I'd like you to meet my mother, Therese."

Before Liz could answer, Mrs. Cross gave a delicate sniff and asked haughtily, "Is something burning?"

7

Liz couldn't scrape the carbonized cookies from the baking sheet, so she hurriedly threw a dozen more dough balls onto a clean sheet, slapped them into the oven, and set the timer. Dashing back to the sitting room, she tried to remind herself that Mrs. Cross, despite her leonine appearance, was human. Surely she would understand—maybe even empathize—with Liz's crazy moment.

Instead, a cool gaze met her at the sitting room door. Was Jackson's mother counting the coffee spots on Liz's pants?

Lose the nerves, Liz. Summoning her most gracious smile, Liz walked to the sofa, where the Crosses sat side by side. "Now that I've taken care of the cookie emergency, perhaps we can begin again. Welcome to Pleasant Creek, Mrs. Cross. I hope you have a wonderful time here. Fresh cookies will be ready in a few minutes, but in the meantime, may I get a cup of coffee for you? I also have a variety of teas."

"Do you have dark chocolate-toffee-almond biscotti coffee? No, I don't suppose you do." She sighed and rubbed her perfectly smooth forehead.

"Mom lives in Seattle, the gourmet coffee capital of the world," Jackson told Liz, with a clearly forced chuckle. "You can find purple potato lattes there."

When Mrs. Cross didn't smile, Liz steered the conversation to a different subject. "I've always wanted to visit the Northwest. It must be beautiful."

For a moment, her carefully made-up face brightened. "Seattle is wonderful. I love the mountains and the ocean." Then her expression became derisive again. "So much more interesting than miles and miles of flat cornfields and soybeans. And boring little towns."

Jackson had been born and raised in Pleasant Creek. If his mother had lived here, she had obviously hated it. Liz chose her words carefully. "I'm originally from Boston, so I sometimes miss the ocean. And the city. But I've grown to love the Midwest, especially Pleasant Creek. Indiana is like the nice boy next door—the best thing that could ever happen, but not obvious at first glance."

The minute she said it, Liz's brain hiccupped. Would Jackson's mother interpret that as—

Yes. Mrs. Cross's eyes shone cold, brilliant green.

Heat creeping up her cheeks, Liz murmured, "I'd better check on the cookies."

"Yes. Perhaps you'd better." A smile curved Mrs. Cross's thin lips, the first Liz had seen.

If she was lucky, she wouldn't see another. Liz dashed to the kitchen in time to pull perfect cookies from the oven. Arranging them artistically on a doily-covered plate, she breathed a prayer, lifted her chin, and carried the cookies back to the sitting room.

Predictably, Mrs. Cross refused them. "Airport food does destroy one's digestion. And those snacks they served in first class weren't first class at all."

"These cookies look delicious," Jackson said firmly. He proceeded to down half the plateful. "Mmm. Even better than the ones you baked yesterday."

Liz smiled gratefully at him.

"Jackson!" Crystal zipped into the room as if she wore skates.

He gagged mid-cookie.

Crystal forced herself between Jackson and his mother. Watching Mrs. Cross's frozen outrage, Liz had to cough to disguise her laughter.

Am I such an evil woman, now, Mrs. Cross?

That Crystal might prove an asset at coffee hour had not crossed Liz's mind. After introductions, like a spectator, she relished the fireworks from a safe distance.

Settling herself in, Crystal began her usual monologue about her career. Mrs. Cross tried to draw his attention back to herself, occasionally demanding Jackson's response to a memory only they shared. Liz had never seen Jackson rattled, but after a while, the female tug-of-war began to take its toll. Occasionally, he aimed a silent appeal toward Liz.

Poor guy. Liz attempted to rescue Jackson by hinting at attractions he and Mrs. Cross might visit so that at least he'd be rid of Crystal. Liz even sent Jackson a text he could claim as a town emergency.

But Mrs. Cross would have none of it. "You *are* going to take the afternoon completely off, aren't you, dear? After all, it isn't every day your mother visits you."

Jackson remained silent, but Liz read his mind: *Lucky me.*

Crystal chattered on. Nothing, it seemed, could pry him from the women's clutches.

Liz puzzled over Mrs. Cross's insistence upon sabotaging every escape Liz offered. When Crystal had first invaded their space, she'd reacted as any sane mother would. Yet now, Mrs. Cross didn't welcome chances to rescue her son from a shallow flirt. Her attitude made no sense. Unless . . . Mom preferred the shallow flirt to Liz?

How could Mrs. Cross make that kind of judgment? She'd known Liz only an hour.

Before Liz could explode, Toni's worried voice interrupted from the doorway. "Oh, am I late? I'm so sorry. I thought coffee hour started at four thirty."

Pasting a smile on her face, Liz poured on the positive, ushering the woman to the coffee machine. "No worries. We don't run coffee hour with a stopwatch here. So glad you could make it." As Toni continued to babble a dozen incoherent apologies, Liz turned to the others. "Crystal, Jackson, Mrs. Cross, I'd like to introduce you to Toni McIntyre. Her group is arriving tomorrow. They're hosting a booth at FebFest."

"Great!" Catching his captors off guard, Jackson leaped from the sofa and shook Toni's hand. "I'm Jackson Cross, the mayor of Pleasant Creek. What group do you represent?"

Toni stuttered. "We're the—um, the Sunshine Sisterhood."

"What kind of group is it, Toni?" Liz asked, attempting to bring the reticent Toni out of her shell.

"It's—it's a women's club. We get together to do fun things. Go on little adventures, like this one. There are groups organizing all around the country."

"Well I think that sounds lovely. I have a group of women friends too, and they mean the world to me."

Toni gave a shy smile. Then she immediately fled the room when Crystal rolled her eyes.

Mrs. Cross suggested she and Jackson leave as well—but not before inviting Crystal to dinner with them.

When they'd gone, Liz returned to her quarters and flopped onto her bed. But she refused to assume a fetal position. What had she done—other than burn six cookies—to make Mrs. Cross take such an instant dislike to her?

Recalling her absurd invitation and the expression of sheer horror on Jackson's face, Liz couldn't help but snicker. How would he endure the entire evening with those two, poor man?

Thankfully, Liz would spend hers with the Material Girls, enjoying her friends' company as they put the finishing touches on their FebFest quilt. They had also invited Toni, who had holed up in her room after Crystal's insensitivity. But Toni, who could have enjoyed quilting with new friends this evening, had placed herself in solitary confinement.

Liz sat up. No way would she leave her guest to brood, alone and miserable.

She ran a brush through her hair, left her quarters, and ascended the stairs to the Amish Room.

"Toni," she called softly.

No answer.

"Toni, I'd really like you to go with me to Sew Welcome tonight. Sadie and Mary Ann are looking forward to quilting with you. The other Material Girls would love to meet you too."

Slowly, the old brass doorknob turned. Even more slowly, the door opened a crack. "Will Crystal be there?"

I hope not. "I don't know, but I kind of doubt it."

"I do too." Toni opened the door wider. "She's probably too busy sinking her claws into the mayor."

Ignoring her own irritation at Crystal, Liz urged, "Then you'll come with me?"

"Okay." A miniscule smile stole across Toni's face. "I was looking forward to your session."

The smile bloomed when Mary Ann and Sadie welcomed her. After introductions, Opal, Naomi, and Caitlyn soon were chatting away with her guest.

Thank you, Liz mouthed to the other Material Girls, who had always made her, a newcomer, feel so at home in Pleasant Creek, and did the same for others.

Mary Ann spread the FebFest quilt—with its silhouettes of ice skaters against a silvery, snowy background and starry night sky—on the workroom's big table.

Toni gasped. "What a lovely concept. And beautiful work! Thanks for showing it to me."

"Oh, you don't get off that easy, honey." Sadie stuck a hand on her hip. "You're going to help us put the finishing touches on this number tonight so we can raffle it off over the weekend."

Toni actually dimpled and joined in. She possessed quilting skills most guests didn't, and with each passing minute, the others began to see the shy but pleasant woman emerge from her bog of insecurity and anxiety.

Until Crystal walked in.

Her glittering smile was missing, and Liz guessed that her time with the Crosses had not proven as satisfying as she'd anticipated. Seeing Toni's face freeze, Liz steered Crystal toward Caitlyn, with whom she had the most in common.

The young nurse erased Crystal's frowns with compliments about her athleticism. The skater admired Caitlyn's apple-red hair: "How do you get it that perfect shade? I'm scared to let anyone touch mine, other than a purple streak or two."

As they chatted and laughed, Caitlyn deftly maneuvered the skater toward easy tasks like pressing fabric squares for the Material Girls' spring project—which kept Crystal's attention for perhaps seven minutes. Soon, having spent another ten minutes texting, she breezed out, saying she needed to take care of something important.

With Crystal gone, conversation flowed more freely as they worked. The Girls exchanged the usual Pleasant Creek marrying-and-burying news. As they devoured Naomi's decadent cinnamon rolls, the talk turned to Verena's murder, the Suters, and how Amity had made the terrible ordeal more bearable for the family. Liz learned that several years before, Amity's fiancé had dumped her for a younger woman.

"She could have stayed bitter when he married that prettier young woman." Sadie's eyes sparked. "Instead, Amity helps everyone in need."

"She's been a real friend to Jerusha through all this." Opal pinched a bite from her roll and popped it into her mouth. "Amity's helped with laundry, cooking, and taking care of the Suters' parents—not to mention getting the house ready for the dozens of people who will come to the viewing." She licked a dollop of icing from her finger. "The boys identify more with Amity than Jerusha. I'm sure she's been a comfort to them."

"I'm not sure Jerusha could have handled everything alone," Mary Ann said.

The other women murmured agreement. Given the workload of the average Amish woman—plus strict definitions of male and female tasks within the sect—Jerusha had inherited gigantic responsibilities.

"Part of that is her problem," Sadie sniffed. "Jerusha could find fault with a saint."

"I'm afraid that's true." Mary Ann shook her head as she added more cream to her coffee. "As community-minded as Amish women are, they may not have hurried to ease her burdens."

Liz cast a glance toward Toni, who'd said little during their refreshment time. "Do you know Jerusha? I thought I saw you talking to her this afternoon at the grocery store."

Toni put down her fork. "She . . . likes to quilt. Over the years, I've seen Jerusha at quilting events."

"Which ones?" Naomi asked, and as their talk veered away from Jerusha and toward quilting and judges, Liz watched Toni's face relax again.

Had the chronic critic found some way to bruise Toni too? Perhaps Jerusha's weapons inflicted even worse injuries than bruises . . .

With their new friend's help, the Material Girls finished and pressed the quilt. Liz hugged herself, proud to have participated in this project. The exquisite fabrics and meticulous workmanship almost made the graceful skater silhouettes come alive.

"I'll bet this one goes for a record price." Caitlyn smoothed its folds.

Liz could almost see Mary Ann's inner accountant adding up

figures. Her friend said, "I hope so. Our charity fund could use a boost."

Liz thanked Toni. "I'm so glad you changed your mind."

"Thanks for talking me into coming." Toni's smile broadened, then faded. "Sorry to bail out before cleanup, but I have phone calls to make."

"You are a guest, after all." Liz waved to the woman as she left, wondering at her sudden change in mood. Liz hoped everything was all right. Toni might have personal problems she didn't want to discuss. Had Toni sought refuge in this getaway, only to be harassed by a former spouse or boyfriend?

Stop. Liz corralled her thoughts. While she enjoyed her hobby of analyzing guests, sometimes she needed to mind her own business.

However, with Toni's departure, Sadie made no effort to do the same. "I saw that Jackson's mother came to coffee hour today. Sort of a 'Cross'"—she chuckled at her own joke—"between ice cream and vinegar, isn't she?"

"That's not very nice," Mary Ann protested feebly.

But Sadie had nailed it. Therese Cross did indeed resemble a vinegar milkshake.

Liz tried to keep her voice neutral. "Did Therese grow up in Pleasant Creek? How long did she live here?"

Opal answered, "She was from Chicago. She stayed here until her husband died when Jackson was in high school."

"And she hated every minute," Sadie added. "She made sure everybody knew it too."

As she gathered scattered pins from the floor, Liz said, "Jackson certainly looks like his mother."

"He owes her his good looks, that's for sure," Opal, folding fabric, agreed. "Otherwise, Jackson is exactly like his dad. Richard Cross grew up in Pleasant Creek and never wanted to live anywhere else."

"He was a kind, friendly man who cared about this community," Mary Ann continued the tribute. "He encouraged other small businesses around here. Rich never ran for mayor, but he should have."

"Therese would have killed him." Sadie made a face.

"Why does she seem to be at odds with Jackson?" Liz asked. *And why doesn't she like me?*

Mary Ann obliged her. "When Therese decided to move out west, she didn't anticipate that her sweet, compliant Jackson would object."

"Boy, did he ever," Sadie exulted as she swept. "Kicked up such a fuss that she arranged for him to stay his senior year with relatives and graduate here. But that's when it really went down."

"When what went down?" Liz asked.

Opal sighed. "Knowing Therese's controlling tendencies, Richard had set aside money for his son that she couldn't touch. Unfortunately, Jackson couldn't access it until he turned twenty-one. Therese threatened to withdraw support for college if he didn't attend one out where she lived. Jackson decided to stay in Indiana anyway. He earned scholarships and worked until he received his inheritance."

Wow. "Thanks. That explains a lot." If Jackson and his mother still sparred over Jackson's college choice over twenty years ago, it made sense that they'd disagree about everything—and everyone, including Liz.

So much for not poking her nose into others' business. Liz also forgot it completely when she made rounds of the guest rooms before retiring.

She heard no sound from the Heirloom Room and saw no lights under its door. It was hard to believe Crystal might already be in bed, but she had had a long day.

When Liz saw no light from the Amish Room, she hoped a good night's sleep would help Toni feel better. However, a muffled cry escaped the room as she passed by. Not a small, breathy sob, but a bitter keening, as if the woman's pillow couldn't begin to absorb her sorrow.

Liz's hand rose to knock on Toni's door, but stopped midway. If Toni had wanted to confide in her, she would have done so. Sometimes, though Liz wanted to help, she couldn't.

She returned to her quarters, got ready for bed, and spent the next hour wondering if she should have tried.

8

Jackson rarely called before eight, but this morning Liz answered her phone as she turned sizzling ham in a skillet. "You're up and at 'em early."

"I know you're busy, and I should have called last night," he blurted, "but I was too mad. Mom was inexcusably rude yesterday."

"It was one of my crazier coffee hours," Liz admitted.

"You've got that right. Mostly because of us. And that—that—"

Don't get me started on Crystal. "Today's another day. Hopefully, we'll all have a better one."

"Liz, you're incredible." He exhaled into the phone. "That's why I dare ask you to forgive us. And to give Mom another chance. Would you come to lunch with us at Mama's Home Cooking tomorrow?"

Liz paused so long she almost let the ham share the same fate as yesterday's cookies.

"I know I'm asking way too much."

Though Liz couldn't see his expression, his pleading tone eroded small cracks in her resistance.

"I'd really like you to get to know Mom. She does have some good qualities."

She hides them well.

"I—I want her to see that you're important to me."

Liz sighed. How could she say no to that? "All right. What time?"

"Great! Meet me at my office at noon or so?"

He almost didn't wait for her answer. It was probably good that he hung up quickly, because the moment his voice faded, Liz slapped her forehead. She needed lunch with Mrs. Cross like she needed a mass appliance breakdown and a zit on her nose.

But recollection of Jackson's eager voice awakened the sense that he'd been acting differently toward her lately. She was important to him? He'd never have said that a year ago.

Liz's good mood sustained her through breakfast with the groggy, demanding Crystal and the silent, hollow-eyed Toni.

With ham, cheesy scrambled eggs, and blueberry scones, though, both improved.

"Going back to a power bar for breakfast is going to be hard," Crystal said afterward.

It probably was the closest the skater would ever come to a compliment, but Liz would take it.

———————— *///////////////////////////////////* ————————

"Isn't it a lovely day?" Miriam asked.

Liz gaped at her. "We're going to pay our respects to Verena. How can you be thinking about the weather?"

Miriam smiled. "That is precisely why I am so focused on the beauty of Gött's creation. We view death as natural, within his will. Verena has joined him in heaven. It is an occasion to be joyful."

The sleigh ride seemed to be working some kind of magic on Miriam. Her cheeks reddened and her indigo eyes sparkled as she guided the horses through glistening, snow-covered pastures and country roads.

With the Amish perspective in her mind, Liz drank it all in—red cardinals chirping winter songs on frosted fences, ocean-like waves of snow along their route, and the way the sleigh runners hardly seemed to touch the ground.

When they spotted a puff of smoke from a chimney half a mile distant, Miriam slowed her team to a walk. Liz shifted her offerings of cranberry-nut and chocolate-banana breads on her lap.

Even as they pulled into the Suters' circular driveway, the sleigh-ride magic fled as two others drove up, full of silent people carrying covered dishes and baskets.

"I thought it was joyful," Liz whispered to Miriam.

"It is a quiet kind of joy. We also must respect the family's loss. And this death is a little different because of how it happened," Miriam replied.

Men and boys Liz didn't know—Suter relatives, she presumed—drove the visitors' horses to the barns, while another opened the farmhouse door. Liz followed Miriam and the others into the Suters' front room, where a few additional kin had gathered. Hiram and his sons stood beside the plain pine casket, where the small figure of their wife and mother lay clad in a long white dress. Miriam had told Liz that Verena, like other deceased Amish women, would be dressed in the same apron and Kapp she wore on her wedding day. Though her body had been embalmed at the funeral home and her injuries and autopsy evidence covered, no cosmetics had been used to soften the starkness of death.

Liz stood with her cousin for several moments before the coffin. Miriam's head was bowed slightly as if in prayer. Then she straightened and spoke to Hiram and the boys in Swiss.

The black-clad Suters had donned wooden expressions, though the boys' eyes were rimmed with red. Again, their suffering squeezed Liz's heart, reminding her of Steve. Sometime soon she should call him.

For now, what could she say to help ease these boys' grief? When Liz tried to express her sympathy, they simply murmured, "Dänka."

Miriam led her to another room.

The heavy atmosphere lightened in the practical confines of the kitchen as women, including Amity Bassinger, joined Jerusha in bustling about, preparing and serving food.

Jerusha thanked Miriam and Liz for the baked goods they'd

brought and replied civilly to their expressions of sympathy. Amid subdued kitchen chitchat, Liz asked Jerusha about her encounter with Toni. The Amish woman confirmed that they had indeed met at quilting events and had run into each other while shopping in downtown Pleasant Creek.

But when one of Jerusha's relatives said something in Swiss, she erupted with a flood of words in an invective tone, then targeted Liz in loud English. "So sad that the Kinder must go on without their Mutter. I tried to tell Verena not to go. As her elder sister, I tried to help her see that she should stay home and care for her family. But would she listen? Nay—and she met her death."

Miriam's mouth tightened, and she quietly steered Liz away.

Amity, patting Jerusha's shoulder, drew her to a clump of older women who soothed Jerusha with murmurings in Swiss. To everyone's relief, the hostess's harsh voice dropped several decibels.

Amity offered Miriam and Liz mugs of coffee and showed them the small table with spoons, sugar, and a pitcher of cream.

No smile crossed Amity's round, serene face, but after Jerusha's outburst, her courtesy warmed Liz's heart.

"Have some Bis Zur or Kekse," the woman offered.

"They all look wonderful." Liz couldn't help an admiring glance at the pies and cookies lined up on the kitchen table. A spectacular chocolate cake with exquisite frosting tempted her almost beyond endurance. Instead, she made herself munch a small shortbread cookie.

When Jerusha's voice rose again in Swiss, Amity's gaze followed Liz's.

"It is a hard time for her. For all the family," she said, then excused herself to greet more visitors.

"Amity's right," Liz whispered to Miriam after they exited the house. "I've never met Jerusha under normal circumstances. Perhaps she is not as abrasive as she seems."

Miriam's slightly cocked head and raised eyebrows spoke volumes, but she only said, "Perhaps."

When it was time to go, the young Amish man stationed in the Suters' driveway brought the sleigh to them, but the magic seemed to have deserted it for good today. Instead, Miriam let the horses take them home at their own pace while she gave Liz more details about the Suters' family troubles.

"I've known Verena for many years. She was always quiet and hardworking. How she loved to skate!" Miriam's eyes moistened. "When she married Hiram, I feared things would prove difficult, as everyone knew Jerusha had not wanted him to find a wife."

Miriam had seen little evidence of affection between Hiram and Verena, even during their first years. When conflicts arose between his wife and sister, Hiram tended to see things Jerusha's way, leaving Verena as the outsider.

Miriam, as reserved as any other Amish person, rarely discussed such details outside the community. She certainly wasn't a gossip. Did she too suspect that Hiram and Jerusha had conspired to get rid of Verena?

Then her cousin hesitantly told Liz she'd heard someone had robbed the Suters of a large sum of cash, which had been hidden in a shed on their property, a week before Verena's murder.

"No one heard Hiram and Jerusha openly accuse Verena. But she told her aunt, my good friend, that they were making her miserable with their insinuations that she had taken it. At a quilting last week, she apparently felt she had to defend herself. Verena insisted she knew nothing about the money and certainly nothing about the hiding place."

Poor Verena. How incredibly sad that she'd held no ownership in the farm's financial matters and had been suspected of a crime by her own husband and sister-in-law.

Liz said, "Did Hiram inform the police about the theft?"

She wasn't surprised when Miriam shook her head. "He only talked to Chief Houghton the night of the murder because the chief summoned him."

Liz took a deep breath. "Do you think Hiram and Jerusha killed Verena because they thought she stole the money?"

Miriam's expressive eyes searched the snow-covered landscape as if for answers. "I do not know what to think," she said at last.

But you told me about the Suters because you know I will inform Chief Houghton. Liz's relatives had used this tactic before. Determined not to defend themselves, they hinted to or even outright gave Liz inside information hoping it would reach the police.

Liz said, "I don't know what to think either." She squeezed her cousin's mittened hand. "But I do know Verena's killer must be found."

Miriam's expression didn't change. But the glint in her eye told Liz she would help put the murderer in jail if she could.

When they arrived at Miriam's, her cousin ignored convention and put her arms around Liz. "Thank you for going with me. It was a difficult visit."

"I was glad to go."

After she left her cousin, Liz drove straight to the police station.

As usual, the chief greeted her with an expression somewhere between a grin and a grimace. "Let me guess. You've been out to the Suters' to check things out."

"I went with Miriam to the viewing. She wanted some company," Liz answered innocently. Any trace of levity died as she recalled the visit. "The viewing proved harder to process than I expected."

The chief grunted. "I imagine so. Come tell me about it."

Sitting with him in his cluttered office, she described it and the theft of the Suters' money. Houghton didn't comment, but she knew he probably was weighing the possibility of a sibling conspiracy as she and Miriam had.

He muttered, "I wonder how many other Amish have been robbed and haven't reported it. It's turning into an epidemic, and this thief seems to know his way around the Amish community better than most."

Refusing Houghton's offer of the station's toxic coffee, Liz asked, "Do you think these other break-ins have anything to do with the murder?"

"It seems likely, doesn't it?" The chief poured himself a mug. "Still hard to figure out a connection between a little mouse like Verena Suter and burglaries at the Oertl or Klassy farms."

A mouse. A lump closed Liz's throat as her mind pulled up a snapshot of the small, pitiful body in the pine coffin.

She swallowed hard. "Has anything surfaced in those cases?"

"Not a whole lot." Mercifully, the chief was pretending not to notice her emotion. "The burglars have been careful, just like the killer was careful. No fingerprints. Sam didn't find any DNA or other clues on Verena's body. Hiding her under the ice was a smart move. We sent off some of her clothing for further tests, but we won't get those results back for weeks." He exhaled. "The divers didn't locate anything that resembled the heavy weapon we'd hoped to find. Or anything the murderer would have used to stanch the blood."

She sensed his frustration. "I'm sorry. But thanks for telling me."

He gave her a stern look. "You know I'd rather you'd stay out of this. But we both know you won't. And with you hanging around Verena's viewing earlier, the killer knows too."

She almost asked if he'd received any results on the cupcake left on her porch, but decided not to reinforce Houghton's concern for her. She stood. "I'd better go. I'm expecting a whole bunch of FebFest guests early this afternoon."

"Yes, I imagine you'll be busy. Lots of people coming this year." A sudden twinkle lit his eyes under the fuzzy brows. "You met Jackson's mom, I suppose?"

"Yes. She came to coffee hour." Liz started for the door before she said something unkind.

"Don't let her get to you," Stan called after her. "Jackson doesn't."

Sometimes she missed Boston, where she hadn't lived her life on a stadium screen. But as she drove back to the inn, the chief's advice about Jackson's mother cheered her.

She didn't have to dread tomorrow's lunch with Mrs. Cross. She and Jackson would handle it together.

Thankfully, Crystal had plenty of PR events to attend today. Liz spotted Toni's plain white sedan leaving the inn's parking lot. She waved, but no trace of recognition crossed Toni's face, which wore a mask of dread.

What destination could cause that kind of anxiety? On impulse, Liz turned her Acura and followed Toni's car. Why she was heading out of town, Liz had no idea. Toni had remarked that given the snowy county roads, she was glad all her Sisterhood legwork was based downtown. Toni hadn't mentioned knowing anyone in the area except Jerusha. As they hadn't seemed close, a visit to the Suters seemed unlikely. Did Toni plan to attend Verena's viewing?

Yet Toni was following a route that could lead to the Suter farm. Liz remained a fair distance behind, occasionally driving on a road parallel to the one Toni took. Trying to remain incognito made it difficult for Liz to keep track of the white car, which blended into the snowy landscape. As they drove farther into the country, the side roads narrowed, some never touched by a snowplow. If only she was back in Miriam's sleigh.

Toni *was* heading toward the smoke from the Suters' chimney. She and Jerusha must know each other far better than they'd admitted.

As they neared the Suters', Liz realized she hadn't yet planned a strategy for when Toni stopped there. She couldn't make a second visit to Verena's visitation. Instead, she'd drive past and park a distance away, walk, and try to find a hiding place from which she could observe Toni's comings and goings.

You're kidding, right? Liz's periwinkle-blue parka wouldn't conceal her unless she managed to reach the Suters' barn, but that was currently overrun by their relatives.

The muffled *clop-clop* of horses' hooves awakened Liz from her musings. A sleigh full of black-clad passengers filled the road ahead.

Instinctively, Liz veered to the right—straight into a deep drift, where her car slid to an ignominious halt.

Not only had she lost sight of Toni's car, she had gotten stuck within fifty feet of the Suters' farmhouse. So much for her "covert" activity. Liz banged the steering wheel with both fists.

The sound of the horses' hooves ceased. The sleigh's driver climbed out and eyed the car as Liz attempted to rock her way out of her predicament, spinning the tires in vain.

He approached Liz's window. "You are well into the ditch. I cannot pull you out alone. I will get help, ja?"

If only she could refuse. But her FebFest guests were due in less than two hours. Who knew how long she'd have to wait for the area's lone towing service to arrive?

Liz nodded. "Thank you."

He spoke to a teen boy in the sleigh, and the young man took the horse's reins and expertly guided the sleigh past Liz's car. The Amish man continued to the Suters' house, leaving Liz to desperately hope he would not include Hiram in the rescue effort. Surely Hiram would remain at his dead wife's side. Perhaps her savior would not even mention her predicament to the grieving family.

A vain hope. She recognized Hiram's tall, awkward figure leading a group of black-hatted men, accompanied by another team of horses. Hiram walked to her window, and though his face remained expressionless, his pale eyes shone on her like high-intensity flashlights.

When she remembered to open the window, he informed her that they would chain the back of her car to the double team. The men would push on its hood. Liz thanked him and shifted her car into neutral.

Hiram and the sleigh driver attached chains to her rear bumper, and the driver grasped the reins. Hiram joined the men bracing themselves in front of her car. With a shout from the driver and a mighty heave from animals and men, her Acura emerged from the snowdrift and found its footing on the road.

Liz started her car. The engine hummed, as usual. Liz, exiting the car, tried to think of how to express her gratitude. Should she offer her helpers money? She reached for her bag and opened her pocketbook.

As one, they shook their heads.

Liz flushed, hoping she hadn't insulted them. "Dänka, dänka."

A few men allowed small eye twinkles to invade their solemn expressions. They'd no doubt tell the story of this silly English woman again and again, chuckling into their beards as they groomed horses and fetched wood.

Hiram's flashlight eyes, however, morphed to lasers. She could practically see the gears turning in his head. Why had she come to Verena's viewing earlier? Why had she returned now? She wrenched away from his gaze and returned to her car.

Driving past the Suter house, Liz saw no sign of Toni's car. She did feel the gazes of several women on the porch, though. Liz easily picked out Jerusha, taller than the others. She turned to watch Liz's car as it passed, as if her burning glare could consume it.

You're letting your imagination run away with you, Liz. The Suters surely knew she might simply be driving to a nearby farm.

But the chief's warning bounced off the walls of her mind all the way home: *You know I'd rather you'd stay out of this. But we both know you won't. And with you hanging around Verena's viewing earlier, the killer knows too.*

9

Finally home, Liz grabbed a peanut-butter-and-jelly sandwich for lunch and dropped on the sitting room sofa for a catnap. She loved nestling in this cozy spot with her favorite throw. Drifting off, she reassured herself that here, when her guests rang the front doorbell, she'd hear them.

It felt as if she had just drifted off when the blaring of a horn nearly sent her through the ceiling. Liz stumbled into the foyer, still rubbing her eyes.

Beans, eyes wide open for once, scowled at her as if she'd emitted the blast that had disturbed his nap.

Liz yanked open the front door and did a double take.

In front of the inn, a semi-sized flatbed truck carrying snowmobiles stretched half the length of the block. A big woman wearing a brassy, messy bun and shoulder-length dangly earrings honked again. She waved from the cab and yelled, "Hey, where do I park my rig?"

"That's Bunny." Toni, who had materialized seemingly from nowhere, confirmed Liz's guess. "I didn't know her truck would take up so much room."

As Liz threw on her coat and dashed out the door, she punched her speed dial. "Jackson? My guests drove a semi. My lot's way too small. Is there anywhere they can park it, even temporarily, after we haul in their baggage?"

He asked no questions. "Send them to the empty lot behind the library. Rough pavement and gravel, but it should accommodate a semi."

"Thanks." Liz hung up and summoned a smile as she greeted forty-something Bunny White and her passenger, a long, thin blonde Bunny introduced as Greta Karlson.

"I'm sorry my parking lot is too small for your truck. But after we've carried in your bags, Pleasant Creek's mayor says you can take it to a vacant lot downtown." Liz gave Bunny directions.

"Shoot, we never ran into problems before." Bunny leaned her chin on a muscled, tattooed arm.

"We haven't stayed in a B&B," Greta reminded her.

"I hope your rooms and breakfast will make up for the inconvenience," Liz apologized.

"They will."

To Liz's surprise, Toni had spoken up from behind her. "This inn is way better than any place we've stayed. And Liz makes amazing breakfasts."

"I s'pose I can live with that." Bunny set her brakes and turned on flashers.

"Snowmobiles!" Sadie, who had tramped outside to investigate the sound of the semi's horn, stared in delight at the truck's load. "I love to ride. Just bought a new one last year myself."

Bunny shared her smile. "There's nothing like it. I've ridden Harleys and dirt bikes, but in my mind, a snowmobile tops them all."

Greta agreed, and Liz had to interrupt the enthusiasts to introduce them.

"What are we waiting for?" Bunny asked. "Let's get these bags inside so we'll have plenty of time to ride."

As they carried in the surprisingly small amount of luggage, complications flew at Liz like snowballs. Chief Houghton, ever mindful of constant horse-driven traffic in and around the town, frowned on any fast, noisy vehicles that might cause trouble. Farmers surrounding Pleasant Creek had donated use of their fields for the

FebFest snowmobile race, but apart from those, she knew of no safe place set aside for snowmobilers.

But Sadie would. While the Sunshine Sisterhood members were getting settled, Liz asked her.

"My fields are too small for a group this size," Sadie said, "but the Ringenbergs' farm would work. Let's call 'em."

Liz speed-dialed Opal.

Their friend consulted briefly with her husband, George, then answered, "Sure, your guests can use our fields—the biggest ones on the east side would be best. Not many fences. They can use the woods too. But headlights or no headlights, they have to be done before dark."

Liz thanked Opal, then sprinted upstairs to tell the women.

Fortunately, the idea appealed to them and also to Sofia Lopez, Patti Elston, and Izzy Cunningham, who arrived soon afterward in Sofia's SUV.

Sadie was joining the club on their ride. Mary Ann, whose bucket list did not include snowmobiling, had agreed to stay and keep shop. Caitlyn was meeting them at Opal's farm.

"You come too, Liz." Bunny possessed a knack for issuing commands that sounded like invitations—and getting people to follow them. Was she a combination of Mary Ann and Sadie, but with a Bugs Bunny tattoo on the side of her neck?

Liz had recently seen all the snow she wanted, chasing Toni around the countryside. But she found herself leaving cookies and a note for Crystal in the sitting room. Toni helped her pack the coffee hour refreshments to take with them while Sadie went home to load up her own snowmobile.

Riding with Sadie on the way to Opal's farm, Liz groaned, "Why did I let Bunny talk me into this? What if I break something?" Why did she keep taking opportunities that might result in her wearing a body cast to the Sweetheart Dance?

She texted Opal shortly before they arrived, and a bundled-up George, standing by a road to their pastures, directed Sadie's Jeep, Sofia's SUV, and the semi behind them where to park. Caitlyn already had arrived. Wearing a chic ski outfit, with the afternoon sun highlighting her red hair, Caitlyn could have starred in a winter video.

As always, she readily made friends with Liz's guests. "Thanks for coming up with this awesome idea. Much more fun than organizing my closet on my afternoon off."

The club members eased their four snowmobiles down the ramp and nodded as George joined them and described his land's boundaries.

"We really appreciate your opening your fields to us." Bunny spoke for the group. Sitting in the semi's cab, the leader had appeared large, but now she towered over the other women. Bunny had shifted snowmobiles off the truck as if they were toys.

Fortunately, her giant smile matched the rest of her.

Since they all were gathered in one spot, Liz cajoled everyone into posing with their snowmobiles for a different kind of group picture for the inn's album.

Bunny then shooed the group to their machines, and snowmobiles roared to life.

The riders donned helmets and tossed an extra one to Liz, which she put on. Toni and Patti were lined up at the rear. Caitlyn climbed behind Sadie onto Sadie's bright pink machine—which matched the color of Sadie's Jeep. Bunny, now bundled and goggled, revved her engine. "Hey, come ride with me, Liz." A small knot in Liz's stomach twisted into a bigger one as she recalled a ride with Sadie on her Harley, Pink Penelope. Whatever vehicle she drove, Sadie ignored speed constraints. Did Bunny also believe those limits existed only for other people?

Liz found herself zooming with the others through a surreal white wonderland before she had time to think. She hadn't expected this snow sport to feel like water skiing, but as they bumped over other snowmobiles' paths, Liz recalled the wakes she'd skied over during Julys past.

Liz savored the visual experience of the smooth white expanse before them like a vanilla-frosted cake, as well as the feel of the clouds of snow that showered them like sparkling confetti. Bunny's whooping echoed back with answering yells from the rest of the pack.

Eventually, though, she realized her driver had been taking it easy for the sake of the beginner on the back of her vehicle. Now Bunny ramped up the ride, zooming at rocket speed through the countryside. Apparently, she didn't believe in straight paths. Or using more than one runner at a time.

Then, in the woods, they got up close and personal with several huge oaks and maples.

"Sorry!" Bunny yelled. "They should have cleared this out more, right?"

After snaking madly through the forest, the snowmobiles finally broke out into open field again, this one hillier than the first. Bunny and Liz sailed over rise after rise, Liz clinging desperately to her driver and her sanity. On the steepest rise, Liz's soul—and body—took flight.

She hadn't soared like this since her third-grade crush had dared her to leap from a swing. Liz cartwheeled into the blue sky.

Then she dropped like a rock, facedown, into a deep, pristine drift. *Whump.*

For a moment, Liz's muscles refused to move. Snow jammed her eyes, her nose, her throat. She gagged and coughed. Turning her head to one side, she spat out the snow. She slowly turned over as shouts pounded her aching temples. Thank goodness she'd worn her helmet.

"Liz! Are you okay?" Bunny's anxious face hovered over her. "I'm so sorry. Shouldn't have taken that last turn so fast."

"Don't move a muscle." Sofia pulled a blanket from her backpack and threw it over Liz. The other club members peered at her.

Caitlyn had assumed her nurse persona. "What hurts?"

"Everything." Liz threw her a faint grin. "But I can move my arms and legs. Back and neck don't hurt any more than the rest of me. See, I can turn my head."

"Lie still for now." Caitlyn looked intensely into her eyes. "No dilation. That's good." She yanked off a glove and took Liz's pulse, then nodded as if satisfied. Caitlyn held up a hand. "How many fingers do you see?"

"Three," Liz answered, "and I love your new nail polish. Seriously, I'm good. May I get up now?"

Sofia had been digging around in the snow. "Haven't found any big rocks around here, so I don't think she smacked her head on one. Do you girls see any?"

"Quit fussing over me." Liz pushed herself to sitting position. She grinned. "That was a fun ride! So let's finish it."

On the return, Bunny took fewer chances—to Liz's secret dismay. The hot chocolate and cookies they'd brought miraculously eased her aches and pains. However, her landing had caused a bit more damage than she'd realized.

While they were loading up, Caitlyn reexamined Liz's face. "Your cheek's swollen some, up near your right eye. We'd better put snow on it." She collected some in an empty plastic bag that had contained cookies and handed it to Liz.

She held it to her face, shivering, as she climbed into Sadie's Jeep. By the time they arrived at the inn, the car mirrors told her what she really didn't want to know.

Liz had a black eye.

She was going to show up at the Sweetheart Dance, not in a body cast, but looking like she'd been in a street fight. At the moment, her sore muscles vetoed the idea of moving, let alone dancing, and Liz spent most of the evening on her sofa. She forgot about her aching body, however, when Chief Houghton called her. "Liz, I hate to tell you this, but you need to be on your guard every moment until we find this killer."

"I had planned to, but what makes you say that?"

"The amount of arsenic in that cupcake left on your doorstep could have killed three people."

10

Liz was dreading today's lunch with Mrs. Cross. She made a face as she donned dark pants and a blazer with one of her more sedate scarves. Even the prospect of spending time with Jackson couldn't ease her gut's warning of impending disaster.

Sighing, she turned to her mirror to add a few finishing touches, only to wince at the sight of her face, the right cheek still slightly swollen. Liz added extra makeup to the large bluish-green area under her eye, but she doubted her efforts did much good.

Maybe I'll tell Mrs. Cross I was in a street fight.

Liz chided herself for being so negative. She knew it was partially because fear lurked beneath her angst—fear that originated with that lovely, deadly cupcake.

Well, she refused to let that fear dominate her day. The chief had assured her that his officers would canvass area bakeries and track down the cupcake's origins. She wouldn't think about it anymore.

Nor would she allow her whiny muscles to dictate her attitude. Liz turned from the mirror and pulled on her favorite boots, flinching a little.

Crystal had stayed overnight elsewhere, sparing Liz and the rest of her guests from her prima donna behavior.

Though breakfast with the club members began with a discussion of what Sadie had told them about the stolen quilts, Liz successfully steered the conversation to FebFest fun. The meal ended with a unanimous vote that Liz's blueberry pancakes and sausage were the perfect fuel for setting up their booth.

It was a good day. Why borrow trouble before it happened? Maybe lunch would prove more tolerable than she expected. Perhaps she'd even find something positive in Mrs. Cross.

To bolster her optimism, Liz gave Beans a good scratch behind the ears before she left. He groaned with happiness and gave her hand a tiny lick. Her mood edged up another notch.

Though as she waited outside Jackson's closed office door, watching minutes tick by on the town hall clock, her cheerfulness sagged.

Suddenly she overheard an unfamiliar male voice accuse Jackson and the town of Pleasant Creek of slander. He threatened lawsuits and payback, lacing incoherent allegations with large doses of profanity.

Liz couldn't remember the last time she'd heard Jackson raise his voice. He shot terse words back like bullets: "For the last time, French, you cannot set up a booth at FebFest or at any festival in Pleasant Creek."

French? The name dinged in Liz's mind. Was he the guy who'd tried to pass off shoddy merchandise as genuine Amish products?

"When you can demonstrate quality in your goods and solid business practices, ask again. Otherwise, I will consider any visit from you as harassment, and you will hear from our town lawyer."

Jackson's door burst open. She took a step back as a tall, flabby man with thinning hair and a mustache barged past her, still ranting.

Jackson, eyes glinting like a polished sword, stood in his office doorway, as if daring French to return. She gave Jackson a tiny, timid wave.

The screech of tires drew their attention to the front windows, where they saw French peel out in a big, shiny black van.

Jackson's shoulders relaxed, and a sheepish smile tugged at his mouth. "I'm sorry. Not sorry for what I told that, uh—"

"Skunk. That's what Sadie would call him."

"Good word. Accurate. Anyway, I meant what I said to that skunk, both on the phone and in my letter. I'm not sorry I threw him out today." His flint-like gaze finally softened. "However, I'm sorry you had to see it."

"Don't worry about that." She took his arm. "Lock up and leave it all behind for a little while."

"I'd love to." He checked his watch. "But Mom's waiting for us. French made us late. She'll raise Cain." He cocked his head and, for the first time, his gaze found her bruised cheek.

Liz's heart sank. "I suppose you want to know how I got this black eye."

"I really didn't notice," he demurred.

Liz snorted. "You may be a good mayor, but you're a terrible liar. I went snowmobiling with my new guests yesterday and took a major spill." She looked at her hands. "No body cast. But you may be stuck with a Sweetheart Dance date who looks and moves like she was mugged."

"You'll look wonderful." Jackson smiled. "I wouldn't want to go with anyone else."

"*Please* don't mind me," said a cold voice behind them. "After all, I have heard it said humans can go indefinitely without eating."

Not an auspicious beginning. Liz knew her cheeks had turned bright red.

Turning to his mother, Jackson said drily, "Of course, you're right, Mom. Which is why a fifteen-minute delay shouldn't cause a cosmic problem."

"My, even this far away I can smell that delicious fragrance from Mama's." Liz wedged her words between the glaring adversaries. "Maybe her homemade chicken and noodles? Let's go before she runs out."

At the restaurant, they had to wait a few minutes for a small round table because Mrs. Cross had not remained there to reserve one. Thankfully, Jackson did not point that out.

The cheerful waitress poured coffee and water, and then quickly took their orders. With the efficient service, the small lines between Mrs. Cross's eyes faded somewhat.

"I'd forgotten how good Mama's coffee is," she admitted after a sip or two.

Jackson settled back in his chair. "It *is* good. And Mama's is a great place to relax after a busy morning."

Mrs. Cross's penciled eyebrows lowered, and Liz imagined her thinking, *Busy. Yeah, I'll bet*, as the woman's potent gaze invaded her own. Fortunately, Jackson launched into a brief but forceful account of French's end-of-the-morning visit. Liz hated to see him stirred up again. But was he trying to show his mother that his delay had nothing to do with Liz?

The thought of such a knight-in-shining-armor tactic warmed her.

Jackson had barely finished his story when an elderly woman with a walker made her way to their table. "Mayor, I've tried my best to be patient, but enough is enough." She waved a finger at him. "You have to do something."

Jackson's long-suffering smile told Liz he didn't appreciate the interruption, but he said, "I'll be glad to try, Mrs. Perkins. What can I do for you?"

"It's that blasted daylight saving time. Every year, it upsets my chickens something terrible."

Liz choked a laugh into her napkin. How did Jackson keep a straight face?

Perhaps by glancing at his mother's.

He said carefully, "I'm so sorry, Mrs. Perkins—"

"'Sorry' don't help it." She sent a glare around the table. "Every March, they change the clocks, and my girls don't know when to roost or wake up. They stop laying, did you know that? Every March. All because a bunch of fools got too much time on their hands, so they got to mess up everybody else's schedule."

By now, her rant had attracted the attention of several surrounding tables. Liz noticed grins—and a few heads nodding in agreement.

"The change affects us all, doesn't it?" Jackson said sympathetically. "It's always confusing at first. But chickens are very intelligent, and I'll bet yours catch on soon."

"Well, yeah. The girls are smart—especially Maudie Mae." The old woman's face brightened. "That hen can cluck the whole last line of 'The Star-Spangled Banner.'"

Now Liz ducked her face over her water glass, trying to stop her shoulders from shaking.

"Impressive," Jackson said solemnly. "Maybe the time change gives Maudie and the other chickens a needed break so they can continue overall excellent egg production."

"Well, maybe," Mrs. Perkins conceded doubtfully. She raised her chin. "But I still think you should tell them loafers in Indianapolis that if they want to wreck other people's lives, leave my chickens out of it!"

"I'll let our state representative know," Jackson promised.

"Good." Having said her piece, the old lady gave a firm nod and haltingly made her way to the cash register.

At least Mrs. Cross held her peace until after Mrs. Perkins exited the restaurant. Then, jaw set like a trap, she released her quiet, sibilant question: "So you want to spend the rest of your life—your talents, your abilities—settling *chicken* controversies?"

For the first time, he freed a smile. "It beats being a negotiator in the Middle East."

"You could have been one," she hissed. "If you had only listened to me, you could have attended the best schools, networked with the best people—"

"That depends on how you define 'best.'" Jackson's smile had vanished.

Liz didn't know whether to feel insulted or relieved that they seemed to have forgotten her existence. Maybe she could slip away "to the ladies' room" and sneak out the door. They'd never notice she was gone.

"Think how you spent your morning, Jackson: running an insignificant little furniture factory, arguing with an idiot about festival booths, trifling with an old lady who can't see past her henhouse. It's a shame you have to deal with such ignorant morons."

"French is a moron," Jackson said, his iron tone mirroring his mother's, "but Mrs. Perkins is not. She's a shrewd, hardworking woman who loves her farm and her independence, and she matters to me."

Liz wanted to stand up and cheer. Mrs. Cross's mouth hardened into a line.

A miniscule smile tugged at Jackson's mouth. "Besides, small towns don't possess a monopoly on morons. I imagine Seattle has its share as well."

Their salads arrived, forestalling an explosion from Mrs. Cross. Liz had never been so glad to see lettuce, tomatoes, and croutons in her life. However, every bite caught in her throat. Her tablemates' glares and somehow angry chewing didn't ease the warlike atmosphere.

"But why are we talking only about us?" His mother suddenly focused the spotlight on Liz.

She almost choked on an onion.

"Tell us why you came to Pleasant Creek," Mrs. Cross purred. "You are from Boston, are you not? Perhaps you can enlighten me as to why this little town"—the tiniest drop of venom oozed from the word—"holds such fascination for you."

Liz paused, then answered, "I didn't know Pleasant Creek existed—actually, I didn't really know Indiana existed—until my mother died. When I read the diary she willed to me, I discovered she'd run away from the Amish community in this county. I felt alone in the world—my godson, Steve, had joined the military and was, still is, stationed overseas—and I was tired of corporate life. So I came here to find my family."

"I'm glad that family is so important to you," Mrs. Cross said in a silky tone.

Was she trying to trap Liz in some weird way? "It is," Liz confirmed, then concentrated on her salad.

Mrs. Cross didn't seem content to let it go, however. "Why did your mother run away?"

Liz remained reticent and was pleasantly surprised when Jackson piped up. She let him explain how a young man from a prominent but corrupt Amish family had courted her mother, then threatened her parents and siblings when she discovered his clan's secrets.

"Like something out of a novel," Mrs. Cross murmured.

"High drama." Jackson boasted, "Liz helped uncover the whole operation."

She couldn't help unleashing a smile.

"Yes, I've heard Liz is quite the sleuth." His mother touched her mouth with her checkered napkin.

Was that a compliment or an insult? It sounded anything but a simple observation. Liz steered her involuntary sharp glance away from the table. She couldn't shake the feeling the woman knew far more about her than she'd let on.

Not that Liz had anything to hide. But was Mrs. Cross trying to catch her in a lie? Had she paid an investigator to dig into her background or something?

Liz sizzled at the thought, then reminded herself that suspicions did not equal facts, especially without one shred of evidence to support them.

"Tell me about your B&B," Mrs. Cross urged in that frighteningly refined tone. "Historic houses are so attractive, and yours is no exception."

"Thank you." The less she said, the better.

"But they also can become quite expensive," Mrs. Cross continued. "Did yours require extensive improvements?"

Why do you want to know? "It needed work, but I'm quite satisfied with it. And my guests seem to enjoy the inn."

Fortunately, chicken and noodles came to Liz's rescue, temporarily ending the . . . conversation? Interrogation?

Stop reading between the lines. She managed to swallow a few bites of Mama's delicious dish, hoping it would mellow Jackson's mother. Perhaps they could quickly end this lunch on a civilized note, if not a positive one.

As they finished, Jackson said, "Liz, I'll walk you back to the inn."

A statement, not a question. She cast a curious, sideways look at him and saw deep concern in his eyes.

Of course. He would have heard about the poisoned cupcake from the chief.

"All right." Liz kept her tone light, hoping his mother would not consider this abandonment. One look at her, however, said otherwise.

Mrs. Cross spoke through her teeth. "Jackson, you know I dislike driving on snowy roads. I only drove the rental car here because of your busy morning."

"Mom, you made it just fine." He leaned forward and winked. "Surely, you're not so old that I have to chauffeur you around."

Liz barely kept from slapping her forehead. There were some things no one—not even a handsome, charming son—should say to a woman.

Mrs. Cross's eyes glittered and, grasping her coat and designer bag, she rose to her full height.

Jackson stood too and placed a restraining hand on her shoulder. "Mom, I'm sorry. I shouldn't have said that. Will you sit and listen to me for just a moment?"

She paused, then sank gracefully onto her chair.

Jackson said, "Earlier this morning, I learned from our police chief that a prowler recently left Liz a very dangerous gift."

His mother's eyes widened as he, lowering his voice, described the arsenic-laden cupcake. "My goodness," she said quietly.

"So you see why I must ensure her safety." Jackson had reverted to his concerned-public-servant persona.

It wasn't a put-on, but Liz still smothered a grin.

Jackson continued, "The chief asked that I help keep an eye on Liz, her B&B, and her guests."

"Certainly I understand that," Mrs. Cross said smoothly. "But we can drop her off, can't we?"

Jackson set his jaw—which made him look all the more like her. "No, Mom. *We* won't. I want to talk to Liz alone. Without you sticking verbal pins into her."

Liz froze.

"I am at a loss to know what you mean, Jackson." His mother's eyes glittered. "I came to lunch at your invitation. I have expressed interest in your friend's family and occupation. Is that such a despicable thing to do? But you obviously see me as a villain, so I will remove my offensive presence. In fact, if I can find a way out of this state that does not involve riding horseback, I will be gone before day's end."

Mrs. Cross stood and strode out the door, ignoring the cash register as if it were below her dignity. Liz gaped after her. She was conscious of numerous pairs of eyes on them and the sound of whispers, soft and plentiful as falling snowflakes.

Chuckling ruefully, Jackson picked up the bill. "She certainly does know how to make an exit, doesn't she?"

Liz wasn't about to comment. Instead, she patted his arm. "I'm so sorry this didn't work out."

"A bad idea, obviously." He leaned his head on his hand. "You handled Mom well. Better than I did anyway."

She hated to see him so down. "How about coffee back at the inn?"

He brightened. "That would be a nice ending to a lousy lunch."

After paying, they walked through downtown. The sunshine and fresh air cleared their minds and hearts. They absorbed some FebFest excitement as booths were going up everywhere. Liz waved at the Sunshine Sisterhood members and pointed out several of them to Jackson.

She wanted to forget their disastrous lunch and enjoy the prospect of the festival, but curiosity elbowed her until she asked, "What did you want to tell me?"

"To be extra careful—on the ice and off." Jackson took Liz's arm and pulled her to his side so she avoided a slick spot on the sidewalk. "Also, I'll be checking on you at night as well as day. So look before you shoot, okay?"

"Sadie won't be staying nights with me, so relax." She grinned, trying to ease his worry. "I appreciate your concern, but let's not overreact. After all, the whole Sisterhood club is staying several nights. Anyone who would mess with Bunny or her friends isn't very smart."

Her grin resurrected his. "So I've heard. But I'll still be looking in on you."

Jackson could have told her this within his mother's earshot. But Liz didn't mind that he'd avoided an additional barrage of negatives. Arriving at the inn, Jackson's relaxed banter ceased. He scanned the front and side yards, probing areas in shadow. As they walked toward the back door, he told her, "While the coffee's brewing, I'd like to take a look around inside, as well."

"One more minute outside." She stopped and inhaled deeply, letting the scent of sun on neighboring pines refresh her.

However, she still hadn't brought up a subject that had disturbed her since they left Mama's. "Will your mother really leave today?"

"No." He rolled his eyes. "Mom would never leave when she doesn't have the upper hand. That would violate her principles."

Liz attempted a chuckle, but a new question flashed on her mind's marquee in neon lights.

How long did Mrs. Cross plan to stay?

11

"Well, good afternoon, lovely lady."

After a trying lunch with Mrs. Cross, Liz didn't appreciate the flirty greeting. Nevertheless, she gave the trim, fiftyish man at her rotunda desk a neutral smile. "Mr. Charles Brown?"

"Yeah. Call me Chuck. I'm Chuck Brown." He paused, as if she should recognize his name.

She consulted her laptop. "You're planning to stay three nights, correct?"

"Yep. Me and Wayne Jensen. He'll be in in a second." He leaned forward over the counter, as if conferring a favor on her. "We were *the* quarterback and top receiver on the Ohio State football team once upon a time."

She nodded. "Old friends are the best, right?"

At the mention of the word "old," his eyebrows furrowed. "Uh—yeah."

Probably not the point the ex-quarterback had wanted to make, but Liz, anticipating the egotistical Crystal's return, preferred not to sing Chuck's praises too. She also skipped the photo for the inn album. She'd catch Chuck in a candid shot in hopes of avoiding a big-man-on-campus pose.

Wayne Jensen hauled in his duffel bag and signed the register. Thankfully, Wayne seemed to notice Liz no more than he did the front door. He did, however, notice Beans—not surprising, as the bulldog had draped himself across the entry again. The part that made her stare was that Beans noticed Wayne. Even before the silent man gave him a thorough ear scratch, Beans actually *stood*.

Was that a good or bad omen? She locked her uncertainty away and escorted her new guests up the stairs.

Think positive, Liz. These guys brought only one small bag apiece.

After showing the men their rooms on the third floor, she busied herself in the kitchen, loading several plates with pretty citrus-flavored cookies in bright colors, plus oatmeal-raisin and jam thumbprint cookies, as well as moist apple bread. Yesterday's cookies had vanished within five minutes. Today, the club members had been working downtown and probably had sampled the vendors' fare. Perhaps they wouldn't be so hungry.

However, Chuck and Wayne had brightened at the mention of refreshments, so Liz prepared plenty of food. She'd also tried to prepare for her odd combination of guests by asking Mary Ann to come to coffee hour. Mary Ann had never seen the committee she couldn't conquer. When Liz told her about the current guest situation, Mary Ann listened sympathetically and accepted the challenge.

Now Liz replenished the beverage bar and plumped pillows here and there, as antsy as if she were going on a blind date.

The Sunshine Sisterhood didn't keep her waiting. All six members showed up, so ravenous that Liz feared she'd run out of refreshments before the men arrived. She threw another baking sheet of cookies in the oven, then brewed herself a cup of café vanilla.

"You went to all the trouble to bake these delicious cookies," Bunny said between bites. "Aren't you going to eat even one?"

"I went snowmobiling yesterday," Liz reminded her, "and I ate four then. I haven't done anything nearly so exciting today, so no cookies for me."

"A tough way to live." Bunny helped herself to coral and yellow citrus cookies. "Izzy, aren't you going to even try these? They're wonderful."

Twenty-something Izzy—short for Isabella, she'd told Liz—frowned.

"I had cookies like those at my wedding shower."

The other members assumed patient expressions, except for Bunny, who rolled her eyes. "Izzy, we've talked this through a hundred times. It's been six months. You need to get over that guy."

"I am *so* over him," Izzy seethed, brown eyes snapping. "He was a cheater, a liar, a thief!"

"Then don't let him keep you from eating cookies." Obviously, Bunny's appetite wasn't affected by Izzy's situation at all.

Face blending with her red sweater, Izzy turned to Liz for sympathy. "The whole time Chad and I were engaged, he was seeing someone else. Then he had the nerve to text me the day of our wedding, saying he was leaving me for her!"

If only Liz had made butterscotch bars instead of the wedding look-alike cookies. She murmured, "I'm so sorry. How very difficult for you—"

"It was the worst day of my life. But that was only the beginning." The volume and timbre of her voice climbed. "Chad wasn't good enough to help pay for things, either. He left me holding the bills for everything!"

Greta, Bunny's near-silent friend, spoke up. "Might have helped if you'd sold your dress instead of setting it on fire."

"Oh, you don't understand." Izzy flung back a lock of her long brown hair and sat grumpily back in her chair. "None of you understand."

"Yes, we do." Sofia's large dark eyes were soft with concern. Nevertheless, her voice sounded schoolteacher-firm. "All of us have experienced disappointment, illness, or loss of some kind, Izzy, but that's what our club is all about, right? Learning to make our own happiness and to live life to the fullest."

Jackson came in, with Crystal hanging on his arm. "I met up with Crystal outside," Jackson explained, looking a bit annoyed. Crystal seemed oblivious.

"Did your exhibitions go well?" Liz inquired sweetly.

Mary Ann, who, of course, had been monitoring the situation, moved in on Crystal. Jackson managed to free his arm and fled to the other side of the room.

Liz's friend dazzled Crystal with her own toothy smile. "Everyone in Pleasant Creek is excited about your performance at FebFest. I watched you during the Olympics several years ago. I can't wait to see you skate."

"Thank you." The young woman's smile grew when Mary Ann requested an autograph. Wayne and Chuck moved away from the refreshment table long enough to make similar requests.

Jackson, who was chatting with Bunny, gestured to Liz. She gladly headed across the room.

However, Patti intercepted her. In her understated voice, she said, "That's Crystal Starling, isn't it? The skater?"

"It is."

"I thought so." An odd smile tugged at Patti's mouth. "So it *was* her that I saw a couple of weeks ago at the mall with that Amish guy."

How bizarre. "In a mall? Where? When?"

"In Fort Wayne. I live about sixty miles north, just past the Michigan border, and went to town to do some shopping. I think it was about two weeks ago."

A week before the murder. "What were they doing in the mall?"

"They were talking in the food court." Patti shook her head. "What's weird is that I saw the man downtown this afternoon. It was that guy whose wife was murdered. I saw him on the news last week."

Hiram Suter? The news videographer must have filmed him without his consent, as the Amish strongly discouraged photography that featured faces.

Liz could hardly picture Hiram having a soda with his family at the local drugstore, let alone hanging out at a city mall with a glitzy skating star. And where had Verena been during this little rendezvous?

Unthinkable ideas sprinted through Liz's mind, ideas she couldn't begin to voice. She downplayed the weird scenario Patti had just described. "Crystal grew up here and performed in Fort Wayne not long ago. Maybe he was in town for some reason and wanted to say hello."

"Maybe." Patti shrugged, and joined her fellow club members, who were animatedly discussing where to go for dinner.

Sofia held up her cell phone and showed it around the group. "How about this Indian restaurant? It's only twenty miles away, and we're all about trying new things, right?"

There were a few skeptical looks, but Bunny seemed interested and soon brought everyone around to the idea of curry. They left en masse to get ready for their culinary adventure.

Liz and Jackson left Crystal with Chuck and Wayne and headed for her quarters.

"I need to find some way to thank Mary Ann for rescuing me," he said when they were safely ensconced inside. He flopped beside her on the sofa. "That girl doesn't have arms—she has tentacles."

"I think she just needs to be adored. Maybe she'll transfer her interest to Chuck. He seems more her type." She paused, then decided to take the high road on another matter. "How is your mother?"

Jackson gave her a rueful smile. "She texted me to let me know she's at Once Upon a Tale, browsing through the new releases. When I called her, she said she was buying some books to keep herself busy since I 'seemed to have more important things to do.'" The hurt in his voice was obvious.

"Jackson, I don't know what to say." What woman in her right mind would think anything but the best of this kind, caring, hardworking man?

"You don't need to say anything," Jackson said firmly. "And I tried to talk her into coming here for coffee hour. I thought she should apologize for ruining our lunch. Instead, she insisted we go to a concert in Marion." He eyed Liz. "You wouldn't consider joining us, would you?"

"I don't think that's a good idea." Another session with Mrs. Cross might push her over the edge. Besides, she had something else in mind for the evening. Liz rubbed her forehead. "I've had quite a day."

"Yes, you have." His hand crept over hers. "You deserve peace and quiet. I hope you get it."

"So do I."

After he said goodbye, she watched from the window until his tall figure strode out of sight.

She called Naomi.

"Hey," Liz answered her greeting. "Want to go to Fort Wayne tonight?"

12

"So you're looking for *more* excitement in your life?" Naomi, riding in the passenger seat as Liz drove, shook her head. "Silly me. I thought you might take a break tonight."

"I *am* taking a break," Liz defended herself, "especially when I might have been suffering through an evening with Jackson's mother." She gripped the car's wheel as if it were a life buoy.

"Lunch was that bad?" Naomi's kind voice radiated sympathy.

"Worse," Liz groaned. "Lunch with Mrs. Cross made me want to leave town."

"Supper out and a movie are cheaper than pulling up stakes and moving," Naomi said, "and lots more fun. Plus, I'd miss you if you went. So let's see if these food-court people saw Crystal and Hiram, then forget the whole thing, okay? Just for a few hours?"

"Sounds like a plan." The mall's evening crowd seemed sociable rather than overwhelming. Both she and Naomi opted for Chinese at the food court. When Liz showed the counter employees pictures of Hiram and Crystal she'd obtained from Internet news stories, they conferred quietly, then shook their heads.

Maybe Hiram and Crystal hadn't eaten Chinese. Besides, food-court workers probably served hundreds or even thousands of people a day. Would they remember these two specific faces in the sea of customers? Liz turned toward a smoothie stand to ask its employees. She had to keep trying.

"Oh no, you don't." Naomi tugged her to a table. "I like my cashew chicken hot, thank you very much. Sit and eat. Then we'll show the pictures at other restaurants."

"Okay, *Mary Ann*." Liz made a face. "What would I do without all my friends ordering me around?"

"You'd never catch any killers," Naomi answered, "because you'd die of starvation."

Liz doubted that, but her hot shrimp and broccoli did taste good. Afterward, they visited the smoothie stand, hamburger restaurant, and pizza place, with no luck.

"Doesn't anybody look at anybody anymore?" Liz lamented.

Naomi shrugged. "There are a lot of people who come through this mall."

A gray-haired woman at the ice cream shop proved the exception. "I've seen all kinds, but those two took the prize for weirdest couple yet. Actually, I've seen them twice."

"Twice?" Excitement surged through Liz. "Can you give me an idea of when?"

The woman squinted, as if trying to recall. "The first time had to be about a month ago. I'd just returned to work after back surgery. Then I saw them here again a couple of weeks ago." Her inquisitive blue eyes searched Liz's face. "They behaved okay—better than some who come here. Are they in some kind of trouble?"

"No." *Not yet.*

Naomi added smoothly, "We're writers, doing a story on people who frequent malls. We'd like to contact that couple. Did you catch their names, by any chance?"

No, she hadn't. But Naomi's fib erased the suspicious glint in the woman's eye.

"It's a good thing I know you're an honest person," Liz kidded Naomi as they headed for the movie theater, "because you did that way too well."

"You're a bad influence," Naomi shot back, grinning.

They should have chosen the kids' movie, because the thriller they selected kept them perched on their seats. Several times, an intense action scene nearly sent Liz under hers.

She blamed the scary plot for the uneasy feeling that crept over her. And for the way her heart nearly stopped when something tapped the back of her head.

The missile wasn't sharp. Quite light, actually.

Popcorn? Liz flopped against her soft seat, trying to chuckle.

Naomi whispered, "What's funny?"

No wonder she'd panicked. On the screen, two cars had just exploded.

"Me," Liz whispered back. "Some kid just threw popcorn at me. I reacted like it was a grenade."

Naomi frowned. "This isn't relaxing. Maybe we'd better leave."

Let one popcorn kernel do her in? Liz shook her head. "No, the movie will get better."

It didn't.

Especially as another kernel hit Liz, this time on the neck. Her stomach boiled, but she held her peace. Liz slowly pulled a compact from her bag and pretended to smooth her hair.

It was a stupid gesture, pretending to fix her hair in near darkness? Her fellow moviegoers probably decided she was either an idiot or insane.

But the small amount of light emitted from the film room did illuminate shapes of those in rows behind her. She saw outlines of messy buns and ponytails, of couples stuck together, of heads covered with sock hats and hoodies atop tall and short bodies.

All dark.

All faceless . . .

Stop it, Liz. No teenaged brat was going to bully her into leaving a movie.

When another kernel struck her from behind, she told Naomi, and they moved to seats farther back.

No more popcorn. And, wonder of wonders, the movie plot moved beyond explosions, finishing with a happy ending.

When the lights went up, other moviegoers gathered coats and mittens, called greetings to each other, checked phones, and gave the movie thumbs-up or -down.

So ordinary. So normal.

Naomi was right. Liz was letting this case get to her way too much.

Before going home, they stopped at a big electronics store that stayed open late. Bright lights, shoppers, tuneless music in the background, and no popcorn—great for shaking off the scaries.

"Are you turning into a techno geek?" Naomi kidded.

But Liz knew she understood.

Her friend grinned. "Did you think the bad guy in the movie looked a little like Chief Houghton?"

"I *knew* I'd seen him somewhere!" Liz couldn't wait to tease the chief about ruining the world's economy.

She pointed her key at the Acura, and it chirped a welcome as its lights came on. A faint scent of buttered popcorn wafted Liz's way.

She tensed, then chuckled. How long would that silly theater episode get to her?

Then, as she approached her car door, she kicked over a bag of popcorn resting on the ground.

A penciled note was attached to the bag: *Enjoy. For now.*

———

"Do you think our stalker put arsenic in the popcorn too?" Her shaking hands still gloved, Liz shoved the bag across Chief Houghton's desk. She'd called him at home and he'd agreed to meet her at the station, despite the hour. "After the cupcake thing, does he really think I'm that stupid?"

"He's growing more desperate," the chief said quietly. "We'll test it, of course, but I doubt it's poisoned. Probably a scare tactic to discourage your investigation. Or maybe it was directly aimed at you finding a connection between Crystal and Hiram. At any rate, you're obviously making him uneasy."

"I hope he lies awake nights," Liz growled. "I know I will."

Nevertheless, she could hardly wait to go home, lock the doors, and take refuge in her quarters.

However, when she returned to the inn and walked in under Officer Dixon's watchful eye, Sofia met her in the rotunda. "Is something wrong?" asked her doe-eyed guest.

"Another prank." Liz rolled her eyes, as if it were a minor annoyance. "Somebody put popcorn in my car."

"Not poisoned again!" Sofia's slim hand went to her mouth.

Liz tried to keep her nonchalant tone. "The chief doesn't think so. Is anybody else around?"

"No. After we came home from dinner, Toni got a phone call and left. The others wanted to walk FebFest at night before the crowds come tomorrow. I haven't seen Crystal or the guys."

Instead of returning to her room, Sofia stood shifting from one foot to the other.

Of all the Sisterhood members, she seemed the most levelheaded. Had something else happened?

"What is it, Sofia?"

Sofia hesitated. "Could—could we talk privately?"

So much for going to bed. She turned to Dixon. "Is it all right if we talk in my quarters while you look around?"

He nodded. "I'll touch base before I leave."

Just entering her quarters unknotted Liz's tense neck muscles. As

Liz made them each a cup of tea, Sofia's troubled face relaxed a little.

Liz set a cup on the table before her. "So tell me what's on your mind."

"It's about Toni."

Not surprising. Sofia's roommate had brightened during their snowmobile ride, but she'd remained more or less quiet throughout her stay. "Go on."

"She must have thought I'd left with the others for FebFest, because she was on the phone and jumped a mile high when I entered our room. I saw a quilt on the bed, a quilt she hadn't shown me—not like her, because Toni loves to show off her finds."

So Liz wasn't alone in noticing the woman's secretiveness. "What did she say?"

"Not much. Just whisked the quilt into a bag and stuck it under the bed. But not before I saw that it looked vintage. It was covered with blue, brown, green, and white patchwork stars." Sofia's face hardened. "It matched Sadie's description of one of the stolen quilts."

Liz's heart sank.

"I went to the library to read until Toni finished her phone call, planning to ask her about the quilt afterward," Sofia continued, "but she must have left. I looked under the bed, and the bag with the quilt was gone."

"Did she take her other possessions with her?"

Sofia shook her head. "Everything else is here. So I have to believe she's coming back." Her voice broke, and she looked away until she could speak again. "I know it looks bad, but I just can't believe Toni would steal that quilt. I've known her for years, and she isn't the type."

Liz's gut concurred—yet if Sofia's observation of the quilt was accurate, Toni must be involved in its theft somehow. "Before we report this to the police, let's wait for her to return. I can't imagine how she'll explain this, but let's offer her a chance."

Sofia exhaled, and she gave Liz a grateful look. "That's what I thought. Thanks for listening. Since you've worked with the police, I thought you could help me decide what to do."

Sofia shouldn't deal with this situation alone, especially since she and Toni were good friends. "Shall we take our tea to the sitting room and wait for her? Would you like some cookies too?"

"Good idea."

As they crossed the rotunda, they were stopped by Officer Dixon, who had nothing to report and bade them good night, with a reminder to Liz that officers would be on patrol.

In the sitting room, Liz enjoyed hearing about Sofia returning to college, where she was studying American Sign Language. When conversation lagged, Liz suggested they walk a thousand steps together around the rotunda. Sofia agreed, but Toni still didn't show, so they decided they'd talk to her in the morning.

At least, she hoped they would.

Finally, Liz fell into bed. Embracing her pillow, she lay awake for two hours before falling into a fitful sleep.

When she dragged herself from beneath the covers at six thirty to let Beans out, she found a note taped to her door from Sofia: *I don't know whether I'm more worried or mad, but I think we should call the police this morning.*

Chief Houghton probably had gone home to grab a few hours of sleep before returning for his regular shift. She'd call him then.

Liz let the shivering bulldog back inside. "How should we feel, Beans, scared or furious?"

He dropped in front of the door again, snoring soundly by the time he hit the floor.

Liz aimed a sour look his way. "Enjoy. I have a feeling you're the only one around here who's going to get any decent rest for a while."

13

"I thought Toni would call you." Bunny laid down her fork beside a plateful of chocolate chip pancakes and stared at Sofia.

"Well, she didn't." The dark-haired woman's frown deepened. "What time did Toni call you? What did she say?"

"It was late," Bunny answered. "About two thirty this morning. She said her mother had gone to the hospital and would we please tell Liz—and take care of her stuff if she couldn't get back here. I said, 'Sure,' and turned over." Bunny's shrewd eyes narrowed. "It didn't occur to me that she wouldn't tell you."

When Liz had called the chief this morning, he'd asked Sofia and Liz to keep quiet about this latest development.

So Sofia answered Bunny with a vague, "Guess it's not surprising that Toni would miss a beat, with her mom being sick and all."

After breakfast, though, she brought her dishes into the kitchen and whispered to Liz, "What do you think is going on?"

Liz didn't want to tell Sofia she suspected Toni was trying to escape arrest, although it must have occurred to Sofia as well. "I'm not sure. After you all leave, I'll inform Chief Houghton about Toni's call to Bunny."

Sofia thanked her and rejoined the rest of her group. Liz heard the Sunshine Sisterhood leader cracking the whip and organizing her troops. They left shortly thereafter for the festival to promote their booth.

Liz hoped that FebFest would keep Sofia occupied all day, so she had less time to worry.

Liz called the chief, then tidied some of the rooms, as she doubted the other guests would awaken for a while. Sure enough, Chuck and

Wayne appeared midmorning. Chowing down as if starved, they asked about Crystal's whereabouts.

"Sorry, I don't know." Liz gave them a bright, empty smile. "Crystal opens FebFest tonight, so I imagine she's either sleeping late or practicing."

They muttered assent, and Liz expected them to leave or go back to bed. To her surprise, they cleared the two inches of new-fallen snow from her steps, porches, and walks.

"Thanks, guys." Their thoughtfulness warmed her. Chuck and Wayne might be clueless in some ways, but despite being guests, they didn't hesitate to pitch in.

"Glad to help." Evidently Chuck had given up on Crystal—for now—because he told Liz he and Wayne were off to meet an old football buddy in Indianapolis.

After she and Sarah had finished cleaning the rooms, Liz called her godson, Steve, who probably was nearing the end of his military workday, not quite halfway around the world.

"Hey, Mom!" The delight in his voice faded her worries for a little while.

They chatted for as long as Steve could spare. But all too soon, he had to go. He promised they would talk again soon. After hanging up, Liz continued to explore online auction sites and other possible sales outlets in a vain hope of finding the stolen quilts.

Half an hour later, she gave up and decided to walk downtown, hoping a sample of pre-festival excitement would give her an additional boost.

She'd visit Miriam's booth and maybe grab lunch with her cousin, with whom she could share the news of Hiram Suter's startling rendezvous with Crystal. Perhaps Miriam could shed some light on Hiram's bizarre behavior.

Donning her parka and boots, Liz stepped over Beans, trod the cleared porch, and turned up her face to soak in the clean, bracing sunshine.

Tramping toward the festival, she hoped Jackson remembered that he had asked her to attend the first night of FebFest with him, as well as the Sweetheart Dance.

But that was before Mrs. Cross had shown up. He hadn't mentioned their festival date yesterday. However, with its disastrous lunch and the eventful afternoon and evening after it, yesterday hadn't exactly followed the planner.

The sights and sounds of FebFest would lift anyone out of the doldrums. In the front yards of homes near the town square, some families already had been hard at work, designing snow figures they would enter in the contest. Some creations sported traditional snowmen faces, with top hats and rows of black buttons, but there were plenty of creative ones as well. One resembled an A-list celebrity, and another a popular cartoon figure.

Waves of a hot, chocolaty scent wafted through the crisp air. *Yum.* Naomi was selling molten fudge cakes again this year. Maybe Liz would talk Miriam into having cake for lunch.

She soon saw that the choice wouldn't be that simple. Food booths of every kind lined the town square. Already, the fragrances of Amish booths selling hearty soups, fresh breads, and hot cinnamon rolls blended with those featuring Indiana's famous pork tenderloin sandwiches, as well as Italian and Mexican food.

As always, Jackson and the festival committees made sure that vendors sold crafts of excellent quality. Because of winter weather, woodworkers' booths were featured inside Jackson's large warehouse building near downtown. But other home crafts, such as pottery, home-canned goods, clothing, pillows, and rugs, were sold outside. Liz stopped and chatted with Maya Morrison, who raised sheep and turned their wool into gorgeous ponchos, sweaters, scarves, and bags.

"Is Sadie going to win the Frozen Turkey Bowl this year again?" Grinning, Maya folded a variegated scarf Liz had bought and placed it into a bag emblazoned with a stylized picture of a sheep.

"She says she is, but Caitlyn's promised to give her major competition."

"I'll still put my money on Sadie."

Liz grinned, took her purchase, and meandered on.

She spotted Sadie, Mary Ann, and Opal at the large, heated tent where the Material Girls' church, Pleasant Creek Community, held a fish fry. Liz only waved at them because the food counter's line, consisting mostly of townspeople, snaked outside.

A nearby restaurant tent run by several Amish families also had attracted plenty of local customers. Amity Bassinger worked there like a quiet whirlwind, cooking and serving food, cleaning tables, and supervising girls who helped.

Liz saw the colorful Sunshine Sisterhood booth in the business and organization section too. However, Bunny and Patti, busy handing out literature and talking to passersby, didn't appear to notice her.

Before Liz stopped at Miriam and Philip's booth, she ducked into the town hall, where all kinds of charity raffle items were displayed. Several women were grouped in front of the Material Girls' skaters quilt, hung on one wall.

A well of pride bubbled up in Liz. With its black silhouettes and shimmering night sky and stars, the quilt had to be one of their best. Of course, she hadn't done the most challenging work—Mary Ann, Sadie, and Opal were true quilt mavens. But with her own hands, Liz had helped create this lovely blanket. Had securing any patents, back in the days she'd been a lawyer, given her this kind of satisfaction?

A deep voice behind her spoke. "You and the other Girls really outdid yourselves this FebFest."

Jackson's smile added to her enjoyment. "With Mary Ann and

Sadie in charge, I've certainly learned a thing or two."

They chatted for a minute, and Jackson didn't mention the popcorn incident last night. Or Toni's disappearance. Perhaps the chief hadn't yet briefed him, which was fine. Liz was growing tired of reporting new disasters.

Jackson's question interrupted her musings. "You still up for tonight?"

"Sure, if you are." Liz hesitated. "Is your mother joining us?"

"No. She's mad at me." His grin vanished. "I wouldn't be surprised to see her riding bareback out of town tonight."

"I'm sorry." What else could she say?

"I am too." He lowered his voice. "Our newest quarrel started when Daryl French served me with a notice he's filed two lawsuits: one against the town and a separate one against me."

"Oh no!" Liz's heart sank.

Jackson shrugged. "Both the town lawyer and my personal one say he doesn't have a leg to stand on. But Mom exploded and wanted to call all her big-city legal eagles. I wouldn't let her. She demanded that I resign as mayor. I told her I won't. Anyway, I don't think she's in the mood for a small-town festival tonight. But I am." Now his grin returned, with all its charisma. "Pick you up about six?"

"Great."

He had to go then, but now the afternoon looked even brighter, despite Jackson's bad news. Humming, Liz wove through the growing number of festival attendees to the area where Miriam and Philip had set up their booth.

Rows of delicious-looking canned goods brightened their small wooden structure, along with perfectly baked golden-brown pies and breads. Miriam had also sewn colorful aprons, pot holders, and table linens, none of which she or other Amish women would think of using. But tourists appreciated their excellent workmanship.

Liz greeted Miriam, Grace, and Keturah, the girls bright-eyed and excited about the festival. Philip gave Liz a quiet smile, then went to find his sons, who were exploring the town square.

Liz exclaimed over the lovely understated rugs her cousin also had made. She pointed to one that featured various shades of green and dark blue. "I tend to put all my prettiest finds in the inn, but I want that rug for my quarters." She dug in her purse for money.

Miriam nodded. "I always seem to sell my favorites. But I am glad you will have that one."

She tucked the rug into a bag for Liz, then sent the girls to buy refreshments. Watching their Kapped heads bounce along the sidewalks, Miriam said, "Is something on your mind?"

"You sound like my mother. She always sensed when I needed to talk something over." Liz glanced around, then in a low voice, told Miriam about Hiram Suter and Crystal.

Her cousin's face grew grave. "Though Hiram and Verena were not well matched, I would not have suspected Hiram of that kind of wrongdoing. Rather than bending rules, he tends to encase them in iron." Miriam's frown deepened. "I do know that before he married, Hiram worked for Crystal's father, who owned a construction company. However, I do not recall that they courted, even during his *Rumschpringe* days."

Liz hoped she was right—that no past or present chemistry between the two would have motivated them to get rid of Verena.

Customers began to crowd Miriam's booth, so Liz pitched in until Philip returned with his youngest son in tow. When business slowed, Miriam consented to grab a bite to eat with Liz, and they hurried to Naomi's busy stand to enjoy molten fudge cakes. Times like these always made Liz wish they had grown up together, chatting and giggling as cousins should. But she breathed a silent prayer of thanks that despite hectic lives as adults, she and Miriam always managed to connect.

Before she walked home, Liz stopped by the police station, hoping that if she told the chief Miriam's new information about Hiram working for Crystal's father, he'd update her on his progress in finding Toni or release a tidbit about Verena's case.

When she informed him, the chief rubbed his chin thoughtfully. "That makes things a little worse, doesn't it? A past connection between those two, and no alibis that can be confirmed."

"Any progress on finding Brett Landry?" Liz prompted. "Or anyone who saw Hiram the afternoon of the murder after he left his farm?"

"None, I'm afraid. We checked the other local B&Bs where Landry, Crystal's supposed alibi, might have been staying. No one had heard of the guy or could put her description of him with a name. Ditto for the local motels. So he probably gave her a false name, and I haven't been able to dig up anyone else who saw him or his car. But that doesn't mean I won't keep trying." Stan's eyes glinted. "I'd really like to know why that guy just happened to be walking the lake path the afternoon of the murder. If he even exists."

"Anything new on Toni?" Liz both anticipated and dreaded his answer.

"I talked to Bunny White over at her booth earlier today and got Toni McIntyre's mother's name. Lives in Coldwater, Michigan. She isn't sick, let alone hospitalized."

So Toni had lied. Liz's stomach twisted.

He continued, "Thanks for giving me Toni's license number. That's helped us out too. An Indianapolis convenience store's camera caught her car at their gas pump this morning. So we know she headed south, in the opposite direction from her mother. So far, Toni hasn't turned up at the Indianapolis airport or anywhere else. But I put out an APB in Indiana and Kentucky, so we'll catch her soon, I expect."

Liz took her leave and headed home, saddened. If only she could come up with a good explanation for Toni's actions.

She stepped up onto the front porch, then opened the front door and managed not to trip over the ever-slumbering Beans. Good. No one had disturbed his beauty sleep. Liz kicked off her boots and placed them on the mat, then shrugged out of her coat. She crossed the foyer and walked into the rotunda toward the utility room, intending to hang up her coat. Her skin began to prickle.

Someone had come up silently behind her.

Liz tensed, readied her bag to smack an intruder, and whipped around.

It was Mrs. Cross, wearing a singularly unpleasant smile.

A different kind of intruder, but an intruder nonetheless. Where had she been lying in wait? Liz loosened her grip on her bag and forced a pleasant expression. "Hello, Mrs. Cross. Is there something I can do for you?"

"Yes." She raked Liz with her gaze. "Yes, there is. I want you to stay out of my son's life."

No more kid gloves, then. Liz could handle that.

"I believe you overestimate our relationship," she said calmly.

"I don't believe I've overestimated your interest in Jackson. I'm sure you think you are good for him—the perfect partner for a small-town mayor." At her last sentence, her mouth puckered. "But he should be so much more. Deep down, you know that."

"Do I?" Liz summoned a smile of her own. "I believe Jackson feels entirely fulfilled here in Pleasant Creek, doing what he does. As do I."

"Which is why you are so completely wrong for him. You, who left Boston to come to this—this backwoods burg, reinforce his being content with something worse than mediocrity. You do not challenge him to do great things."

That depends on your definition of "great." Liz lifted her chin, but said nothing.

"And all that nonsense about coming here for *family's* sake." Mrs. Cross all but spat out the words. "If family mattered to you, you would not influence Jackson to stay here. You would not keep him thousands of miles away from the only real family he has."

Stung, Liz said, "As I understand it, Jackson made up his mind to stay here long before I ever set foot in Pleasant Creek. You could move back to the Midwest, you know. To Chicago, if you can't stand small towns."

That horrible smile again. "I'm afraid that would never work."

Of course it wouldn't. Mrs. Cross was right. The only way her son would ever live near her would be if dear, thoughtful Jackson felt obliged to care for her as she aged. Because despite her impossible nature, she was his only family.

Liz straightened. "Mrs. Cross, I believe you should go now."

"Yes I should. I have important business to take care of." She turned and stepped daintily over Beans, then left.

Liz stood motionless, still clutching her coat.

Finally, she hung it up and went to the sitting room. She stirred the fire and added wood, then dropped onto the sofa and watched the flames gleefully overwhelm the logs.

Get up, Liz. Don't let that woman disable you.

She donned her boots and parka again and attacked the snow covering the path to the gazebo, which Chuck and Wayne hadn't done. Once at the gazebo, she scraped and flung shovelfuls off benches and the floor. For an infinitesimal moment, thoughts of the cupcake and popcorn episodes poisoned her mind, reminding her she was alone. But she was too angry to be afraid.

Come and get me, stalker. I'll smack you to the moon with my shovel.

Sweating and exhausted, but feeling much less tense, Liz returned to the inn and plopped onto the sofa in the four-season room. A short, sweet nap brought her back to life so she could shower, then bake cookies for coffee hour.

Only Chuck and Wayne showed up. Liz became the sole audience for detailed descriptions of their college football exploits.

When she'd had enough, Liz mentioned Crystal would perform that evening as part of the festival's official opening. Chuck and Wayne left immediately to get good seats.

Two minutes of relief.

Then Mrs. Cross's words crept out of hiding, hunting Liz like feral cats stalking mice.

Ignore them. Ignore her.

Though she'd cover her outfit with a coat as she and Jackson walked the festival, Liz debated on what she would wear. She settled on black leggings and a lavender-and-blue tunic sweater that would go well with her parka and tall black boots.

By the time Jackson arrived, she'd locked most of her thoughts about Mrs. Cross in her mental freezer.

Thankfully, he didn't mention his mother as they made their way toward downtown, savoring the magic of a clear February evening in Indiana.

Upon its exit, the sun already had left colorful orange, pink, lavender, and purple banners strung across the twilight. The town's streetlights came on as Liz and Jackson approached the festival. Most owners had decorated their booths with strings of tiny white lights that shone on the snow, transforming downtown into a fairyland.

Walking with Jackson, laughing and talking, greeting friends and checking out booths, Liz even managed to put worries about subjects like theft and murder into deep storage as well.

At their church's tent, they ate expertly fried bluegill, a specialty the fishermen in their congregation caught and froze during summer for FebFest. With french fries and creamy coleslaw, Liz thought she could eat no more—until one of her church friends informed them dessert was a warm slice of Mary Ann's apple pie with vanilla ice cream.

Then she and Jackson, along with hundreds of other festivalgoers, headed for the temporary ice rink that had been set up in the high school parking lot.

Liz enjoyed Jackson's brief speech, given with his usual flair, and the high school band's spirited numbers. The expanse of ice, however, reminded her of the evening she'd spent with Jackson, the Material Girls, and Miriam's family on the lake—only to end in the horror of finding Verena Suter's dead body.

The sight of Crystal, a glittering vision in silver and red, only added to Liz's unease. Beautiful and glamorous as she glided, the skater looked like the perfect partner in destroying a troubled marriage and plotting the murder of an unwanted wife. Though, try as she might, she couldn't see Crystal and Hiram as a couple.

But they had been seen together out of town. More than once.

With the skater's spectacular leap, seemingly almost to the stars, Liz swallowed her breath. As Crystal performed one impossible jump after another, landing softly as a dove, Liz couldn't help but join the rest of the crowd in oohs and aahs. Such strength and grace could only have been created by a driven, disciplined lifestyle. Did Crystal's clueless manner serve as a convenient disguise?

After the skater finished her routine, she glided to the sidelines, accompanied by a roar of applause. As Jackson handed Crystal a bouquet, she captured him with an arm around his neck and planted a Hollywood kiss on his lips.

Cameras clicked. People stared at them, then at Liz.

Calling for another round of applause, Jackson quickly freed himself as Crystal dropped into more graceful curtsies.

He hurried back to Liz. "Quick, let's go before she takes off her skates."

He grabbed her hand, and they escaped to his office in his nearby furniture store.

"You're shivering. Sit here, in my chair. I'll brew some coffee." He slipped a pod into his machine, clamped it shut, then turned to look at her. "Liz, I hope you realize that I didn't—"

"That was all Crystal. I know you didn't initiate anything."

"I was as surprised as you—though I should have expected something like that. She's stuck in permanent adolescent gear." He shook his head.

Liz tried to smile reassurance, but suddenly, fatigue swept through her. She was so tired of dealing with Crystal, Jackson's mother—all of it.

Tired of shadows that lied and stole and killed . . .

He handed her the mug of coffee and started another. "Maybe while we're taking a break, she'll give up on finding us. We can go back to FebFest and pick up where we left off."

"I'm glad you're an optimist, but if you don't mind, I think I'd rather go home. It's been a long day."

Jackson looked a bit nervous. "Are you sure you're not mad at me?"

"Positive." She looked him straight in the eyes.

Relief eased his tight mouth, but he said, "Something else is bothering you, then. I knew it the moment I saw you this evening."

So much for hiding her feelings. Jackson knew her too well.

She told him about his mother's visit.

Jackson looked stricken, then shook his head. Finally, Jackson took her hands. "I am so sorry, Liz. Please don't believe a word she said. Please. There's nowhere else I belong more than here."

She looked down at his hands holding hers, so strong. So gentle. "I don't want to cause a problem between you and your mother—"

"You're not the problem," he said firmly. "She is." He drew her into his arms, laying his cheek against her hair. "I'm sorry for all this. You're right. I should take you home so you can get some rest."

She hated how this conflict hurt him, but rather than driving her and Jackson apart, Mrs. Cross's opposition only seemed to bring them closer.

Liz felt his heartbeat pick up as Jackson said, "And then I intend to talk to my mother."

———— ⁄⁄⁄⁄⁄⁄⁄⁄⁄⁄⁄⁄⁄⁄⁄⁄⁄⁄⁄⁄⁄⁄⁄⁄⁄ ————

Breathe. Breathe. Again.

Liz lay on the sofa in her quarters. Hopefully, the soothing string quartet music playing softly on her radio would help untangle her thoughts and ease muscles that still ached from the snowmobile incident.

She must have dozed off—how long ago? She had no idea. Her phone's ringing prodded her to consciousness. Jackson? Liz wasn't sure she wanted to hear about the Crosses' confrontation.

But it was Chief Houghton. "I thought I'd let you know that Toni was picked up near Louisville. Apparently, she's singing like a canary and telling everything she knows. They're bringing her back here. But Toni's not the only one who was arrested."

Liz sat up. "Who else?"

"Jerusha Suter." His voice held a note of triumph, his usual mode when he made an arrest, but also melancholy, which came in when he'd had to arrest someone he knew. "Toni told me Jerusha has been stealing quilts from others in the community, then selling them through Toni. I took a warrant to the Suters' house. Jerusha was there, and sure enough, I found two stolen quilts hidden in her room. But that's not all."

"What else?" Liz asked, not sure she wanted to know.

"Hiram's youngest boy broke down and told me Jerusha had threatened his mother the week before the murder. Then threatened him if he told."

14

The next morning, Sofia's dark-eyed gaze met Liz's across the dining room table.

Sofia knew.

Maybe not the details of Toni's arrest, but she knew her roommate was in serious trouble.

Meanwhile, Bunny, alternately issuing orders and jokes, was rallying the Sisterhood over Florentine sausage-egg casserole and fruit cups. She possessed a real gift for inspiring the group with her monologues.

Liz waited for a break so she could accomplish her dreaded task. But Bunny never stopped to take a breath.

Fortunately, Izzy upset her coffee, and while the others were helping her sop up the spill, Liz seized the floor.

"I know you've all been concerned about Toni and her mother," she began.

Patti leaned toward Liz. "Yeah, I miss Toni. Have you heard from her? Is her mom better?"

This is even worse than I thought. "Well, the good news is that Toni's mom is fine. The bad news is that she never was hospitalized. Toni fabricated that excuse."

"What do you mean, fabricated?" Izzy demanded. "You're saying she lied to Bunny?"

"I'm afraid so." Liz told them about the stolen quilts, Toni's arrest, and her implication of Jerusha. "It appears that they've been running an efficient business the past year or so. Jerusha stole the quilts and used Toni as her fence."

A chorus of gasps sounded, then dead silence. For once, even Bunny was speechless.

Liz continued, "I'm telling you this because Chief Houghton will come by an hour or so before coffee hour to interview you."

"I won't do it." Izzy stuck out her chin. "I won't help put Toni in jail. None of us should. We're the Sunshine Sisterhood, remember?" She scowled at Sofia. "Why did you blab about the quilt? You know Toni was just trying to make ends meet."

"Stop it, Izzy." Bunny's voice turned to steel, then gentled. "I know how you feel. Toni has had a rough time, with her home being foreclosed and all."

"And her sneak of an ex-husband." Izzy still glared at Sofia, as if Toni's misfortunes were her fault.

"True." Bunny's eyes moistened. "I wish she would have let us help her, but she wouldn't. Still, whatever happens, we need to be there for her." Her voice hardened again. "Withholding information or lying to the police won't help Toni."

"Chief Houghton is a fair, caring person," Liz added. "If Jerusha coerced Toni into this, he'll sniff that out." The others murmured approval, and Izzy's expression lessened in its ferocity.

"I'll check with the police about when we can visit Toni," Bunny said. "Until then, we have a booth to run. A message to share." She gestured with her head. "Let's go."

As one, they stood and left to ready for their day at FebFest.

Thank goodness that was over, and that Chuck and Wayne hadn't risen early to hear this difficult revelation. Liz scrambled to clean up for that second shift. She took another casserole out of the oven—a non-Florentine version of the sausage-and-egg dish, as Chuck had informed her quite succinctly that neither man liked spinach. The two slumped in at their usual time, yawning and expecting her to pour their first cup of coffee. They devoured the entire casserole, so none was left for Crystal.

Liz resolved to fix Crystal a nice, fattening omelet to accompany the muffins. If she got up before noon.

After the men finished breakfast, they rose. Chuck thanked her for the breakfast, then told her not to expect them back until late. "We'll hit FebFest, then go snowmobiling at the state park," he exulted. "Nothing better than that. Except football, of course."

Liz waved goodbye and whipped through her chores. Sarah was needed at her mother-in-law's booth at the festival, so Liz had given her the day off.

There was no sign of life from Crystal's room. Liz fixed a covered plate of muffins and fruit, and left them with a note on the dining room table.

When she'd finished, she tramped toward downtown. But not to the festival.

This time, her steps took her to the town jail to see Jerusha.

Liz entered through the heavy glass doors. Officer Gerst, who seemed to know the details of Jerusha's case, welcomed her. The female dispatcher searched Liz and took her to the stark visitors' area. She sat on a hard, metal chair inside a cubicle, facing a sheet of unbreakable glass.

"Good luck with this one," the dispatcher whispered. "I'm surprised the chief let her talk to you." He hadn't, but the dispatcher didn't need to know that. "The woman refused to put on prison clothes and won't eat."

This day was just full of fun moments. Liz sent a prayer aloft for patience and understanding.

One look at Jerusha's gray, chiseled face against her Amish black, and Liz knew only divine influence could penetrate this woman of stone. Her blank eyes looked past Liz.

Liz picked up the cubicle's phone. "Jerusha? I'm Liz Eckardt. Remember, I came to Verena's viewing with Miriam Borkholder?"

Zero response.

Liz held the phone away from her mouth and raised her voice. "I want to help you. Would you pick up the phone, please?"

The woman didn't move a muscle, but a scornful glint touched her eyes.

So Jerusha could hear her.

Liz tried to express empathy for Jerusha's refusal to put on orange prison garb. She kept her few questions about the stolen quilts low-key. Could a mix-up have occurred at a sewing session? Could Jerusha have inadvertently taken the quilts home and stacked them with her own quilts or sewing projects?

No response.

"Is Toni McIntyre telling the truth about fencing quilts for you?"

Silence.

Not surprising, as most Amish held the view that they should not defend themselves—especially to an outsider and a former lawyer.

Jerusha continued to ignore Liz's overtures until Liz asked, "Won't you miss your family?"

The woman's lip curled. "No. They will have no one to cook and clean for them. *They* will miss *me*."

"Really?" Kindness hadn't worked, so now Liz aimed a pointed question at the woman. "The boys will miss you?"

Jerusha's eyes sparked. "They are *vёschta*, spoiled as their mother was. They say I threatened one of them. They say I threatened her. Gött knows that only the rod would drive foolishness from their hearts. But Hiram would not listen."

"You struck them? Beat them?"

The stone face again.

"Did you kill Verena?"

For a moment, the chiseled mouth didn't move. Then Jerusha said, "Gött is the giver and taker of life. He knows."

This time, her stern, glowering gaze shook Liz. However warped her attitudes toward Verena and the children, Jerusha seemed to believe the Amish foundational tenet that God alone should control His gift of life.

Was she innocent, yet clinging to the Amish belief she should not stand up for herself in any situation? Or did she refuse to defend herself because she had committed murder?

When Liz shifted her questions back to the stolen quilts, hoping Jerusha might respond to a lesser issue, the woman gave her the same hot-iron look. "Gött knows," she said, then turned her face away.

Finally, Liz rose to leave. "I hope you will talk to the police about what you know. And please eat something."

Again, that curl of Jerusha's lip.

Officer Gerst escorted her out. Liz was more confused than ever.

Earlier, she'd intended to call Rob Carver about Jerusha's and Toni's quilt-stealing enterprise. After all, she'd promised to help the reporter as he'd helped her with Verena's autopsy report. Yet how could she reciprocate, when she couldn't seem to settle her mind about Jerusha's innocence or guilt?

FebFest, now in full swing outside, beckoned to Liz. A band played on a nearby stage. Screaming children careened down a giant slide. Friends of contestants in the doughnut-eating contest cheered them on. Even more booths had opened, and crowds jammed the area so Liz barely could make her way along the town square.

Right now, though, she wasn't in a party mood. She could think only of Jerusha's uncompromising stare and statement of faith. She pushed her way back to the inn.

Liz was stepping over Beans in her entry when her phone rang. It was Jackson.

"Liz?"

She detected a peculiar quality to his voice. "Hi, Jackson, What's up?"

"You—you didn't happen to see my mother today, did you?"

"Um, no. I wouldn't really expect to. Why?"

"She didn't come home last night."

Liz nearly dropped her phone. "Are you sure she didn't go back to Seattle?"

"If she did, she left everything here except her purse. My neighbor saw her leaving yesterday afternoon, just before she came to the inn. Mom didn't take a suitcase with her."

Liz tried to imagine Mrs. Cross leaving her designer clothes behind. Though she didn't know the woman well, that seemed contrary to her persona.

"I've called, texted, and emailed her. I've contacted her closest friends," Jackson continued. "One even told me Mom emailed her yesterday afternoon that she wouldn't be returning to Seattle for several days."

"That fits with what you told me, that she would stick around." Liz didn't add what Jackson had said about his mother's insistence on gaining the upper hand. "Are you going to call the chief?"

"Not yet." He sighed. "If Mom's simply looking for attention, I'd rather not create a commotion. Not until I'm convinced she's really missing."

"Perhaps she took just a few things and is staying elsewhere?" That seemed more like Mrs. Cross. Liz could see her deciding to disappear overnight to teach Jackson a lesson. Liz offered, "I'll check at the other B&Bs if you'll call the motels and hotels around here."

"All right." Relief rushed into his voice. "Thanks, Liz."

What if I have to talk to her? Liz pushed the alarming thought aside. The important issue was helping Jackson.

Surely, as distinctive as his mother looked, they could track her down, even if she'd thought to use an assumed name.

Liz plopped onto the sitting room sofa and summoned her list of other bed-and-breakfast owners on her phone. Because they knew Liz, they bypassed their usual caution about revealing guests' whereabouts. However, none had seen Mrs. Cross.

Liz hoped Jackson had had better luck.

"Okay, what's wrong?" Sadie stood in the doorway, arms folded across her chest.

Liz told her.

Sadie's eyebrows went up. "I thought both you and he would be glad to get rid of that woman."

Liz ignored that. "Jackson's frantic. I've never seen him like this."

Sadie gave her a grin. "That's because you've never seen him when he was really worried about you."

As if he'd heard the mention of his name, Jackson called back.

"Hi, Jackson. Any luck?"

"The fact that you're asking tells me you didn't have any either. Something's wrong. My mother's a pain, and she likes to see me squirm, but she wouldn't pull something like this."

Liz didn't hold the same faith in Mrs. Cross, but this shenanigan didn't seem quite in character for her. "Do you know of any business issues your mother was planning to address yesterday?"

"No." He exhaled. "We divvied up all the property years ago, and she sold everything that reminded her of Indiana."

"Yet, before she left here, your mother said she needed to tend to important business." Liz couldn't help wincing at the memory. "Do you have any idea what she meant?"

"Could have meant anything." Jackson echoed Sadie's words. "She might have said something like that just to set up a grand exit. There might not have been any truth to it."

Unfortunately, that did sound like Mrs. Cross. Liz said, "Jackson, where are you?"

"Just now walking up to your front door, actually."

"Good. Come in and have a cup of coffee." She stood and went out into the rotunda. "Maybe if we put our heads together, we'll figure out what to do."

Jackson entered before she reached the door, his face white and strained. Liz hugged him, and Sadie hugged them both.

"Let's go to the sitting room," Mary Ann called from Sew Welcome's door. "No customers are around at the moment, and it looks like we need to talk. Liz, bring the coffee fixings. Jackson, brief me while I cut this pie. Sadie, we need plates and forks."

Every battle needed a general, and Mary Ann, as usual, had risen to the occasion. Everyone scurried to follow orders. Soon they were seated on Liz's comfortable furniture, Mary Ann next to the door so she could listen for customers entering the shop. For once, her blackberry pie, though scrumptious as always, didn't take center stage.

"Should we call the police?" she asked.

"I'm not sure." Wearily, Jackson rubbed his forehead. "I haven't received any ransom notes or calls. I have to believe she's around here somewhere."

Liz watched as alternating waves of pain and anger twisted his mouth.

"You're probably right," she assured him, though her gut wasn't so sure. "I hadn't thought of this before, but do you know of any old enemies your mother might have in this area?"

His forehead furrowed. "Well, as you can imagine, she made plenty while I was growing up, including some in the business community.

But I've worked to resolve those."

I'll bet you have. How long had Jackson played grown-up to his mother's childishness?

"Therese had some, er, issues in social circles," Mary Ann agreed, "but I can't imagine that after all these years someone would dislike her enough to do her harm."

"Has she made any new enemies since she got here?" Sadie gestured with her head. "Besides Liz, I mean."

"Not as far as I know." Jackson didn't look at her. "Mom really hasn't tried to reconnect with anyone here. Mostly she's done voice and video calls with her Seattle friends."

Liz said, "How about *your* enemies?" Despite Jackson's popularity, no one could please everybody. He seemed to fight an ongoing battle with the sewer board—though she couldn't imagine that any local opponent, no matter how vindictive, would take it out on Jackson's mother.

Then a memory of his recent clash at town hall played in Liz's thoughts. "Daryl French. Could he have something to do with this?"

Jackson threw her an incredulous glance. "French? He's already suing me. Why would he go after my mother?"

"He probably knows he doesn't have a case," Liz answered, "so perhaps that's the only way he can get back at you."

"I suppose my actions and warnings to other mayors have cut into his profits big time," Jackson mused. "I can see him undercutting me businesswise. Or going after me politically. But personally?" He shook his head. "French is the sneaky, greedy kind. I don't think he'd risk jail time just to take revenge."

Something else dinged in Liz's mind. "French deals in antiques, right? And in Amish goods?"

Jackson shrugged. "Largely fake ones—which is why I wouldn't let him set up his stands at FebFest."

"But what if he has even bigger stakes in this area?" Liz cast a look at the others. "What if he's involved in this stolen quilt scheme on a large scale, and he feared Jackson would catch on?"

Mary Ann cocked her head. "Have you seen any evidence of that?"

"None," Liz admitted. "I have a hard time putting him and Jerusha together. Though I can see how he might intimidate Toni. Still, I've learned that criminal activities like these in Pleasant Creek are often connected in some way. Those links may lead to solutions of the big crimes, like kidnapping."

Mentally, she added, *Maybe even murder*, but she didn't voice it. Jackson didn't need that. But could all the misshapen pieces of this disjointed puzzle, including Verena's murder, fit together somehow? What if they were just missing the last few pieces that would make the whole thing click into place?

"I think we should pay Mr. French a visit," Liz said.

"Sounds like fun." Jackson stood. "Let's do it."

Sadie's grin radiated genuine glee. "I'm riding shotgun for this posse."

"No blowing anyone away, dear," Mary Ann said firmly. She pondered for a moment, a perfectly manicured finger tapping her mouth. "Jackson, while you're pursuing French, the other Girls and I might continue canvassing the area for clues to your mother's disappearance. Do you have a recent photo of Therese?"

"Sure. We took selfies by the clock tower." Jackson pulled out his phone. His hand trembled as he swiped through his gallery.

At the sight of his pictures, Liz's throat closed. He'd captured fun mother-and-son moments when Therese wasn't sniping or posing. Jackson himself was grinning broadly.

Bless Mary Ann, she continued in her businesslike tone, "Send it to my phone. I'll print out a bunch of copies. I'll give some to Opal, who's at the church tent, and have her ask customers if they've seen

Therese. Ditto for Naomi at her booth and for me here at the shop. I'll call Caitlyn too and see if she can wander the festival and ask around. Maybe some others friends of yours as well." She lifted her chin. "Don't you worry, Jackson. We'll find Therese."

"Thanks, Mary Ann." Jackson's voice broke. His grateful gaze found her, then Sadie, then lingered on Liz, steeling her to help him.

When the moment passed, Liz said, "I imagine that sooner or later, our canvassing FebFest will draw Chief Houghton's attention. Which brings us back to the original question. Should we contact him? He does have resources we lack, you know."

"But he also knows about the lawsuit." Jackson's hands clenched. "He might try to stop me from talking to French."

Um, maybe he should. Jackson usually kept a cool head. But between him and Sadie, Liz wasn't sure this would work out so well.

Mary Ann brushed away any negatives. "We're still at a very preliminary stage in finding Therese. For all we know, she's made a new friend and gone shopping in Chicago. So let's do this. We'll call the chief later today if we make no headway."

Or after we do. A tiny grin tugged at Liz's mouth. Though she and the Material Girls sometimes frustrated the chief, he always forgave them. Especially if Mary Ann gave him pie.

"Let's take my Jeep," Sadie offered. "It'll go anywhere."

If they needed to remain incognito, Sadie's pink vehicle would prove problematic. Still, they all agreed Sadie was right. They didn't know where their mission would take them.

Jackson fiddled with his phone. "I have French's mailing address, but it's a post office box in Rochester. And I only have his cell number, not his landline if he has one. We may have to call Stan after all, since he probably could track him better than we can. But first, let me try something."

While Liz began searches with her phone for French's street

address, Jackson made a call. After hanging up, he said, "Thank goodness for smart assistants. Scott at the town hall overheard French giving directions to his store north of Rochester, near the county museum."

"Great." Liz jumped up. "Let's roll."

"I'll report anything else we find out," Mary Ann reassured them.

"Thanks." Sadie hugged her. "I need to take care of one thing for a customer. I'll meet you in the parking lot."

Having thrown Mary Ann another grateful glance, Jackson made another call, probably tying up loose ends.

Though Chuck and Wayne wouldn't make coffee hour, Liz put out goodies for the Sisterhood club and Crystal in case their "posse," as Sadie called it, was late in coming back.

Liz donned her old peacoat—far less noticeable than her parka. She reached the parking lot first, so she scraped the Jeep's icy windows. The trailer carrying Sadie's snowmobile was still connected, the helmets in the car's back seat. Oh, well, Sadie's pink Jeep already drew the eye. An additional pink snowmobile wouldn't make that much difference.

Jackson, still white-faced and intense, arrived.

What could she say to distract him, to ease the knots in his thoughts? Small talk wouldn't do it. And the Sweetheart Dance tomorrow night seemed as remote as if it were to take place on Pluto.

"Sorry I took so long," Sadie said. "Somebody always wants to chat when you're in a hurry."

Liz turned to reassure Sadie, but her words died.

Jackson also froze.

Sadie wore a black-and-white faux-fur hat with a skunk's head on it. Its long, fluffy tail waved in the wind.

"Like my new hat?" Sadie, brandishing her shotgun, turned so they could admire it. "I always say if you're going huntin' for skunks, you should dress the part."

As Sadie pulled out of the parking lot, Liz tried to imagine Mrs. Cross's face if or when they found her.

Liz smiled. The thought was one more reason Liz wouldn't quit until they did.

15

On a normal day, Sadie took speed limit signs as friendly suggestions.

Today, she acted as if they didn't exist.

Gripping her seat, Liz tried not to glance at the speedometer. In Pleasant Creek, the police tended to look the other way when Sadie barreled through. The officers in this county, however, wouldn't—especially with a seventy-something driver wearing a skunk hat at the wheel of a shocking-pink Jeep towing a snowmobile trailer.

Thankfully, when they stopped at a gas station, Jackson offered to pump gas and to drive. "Counting telephone poles won't keep me sane. I need to *do* something."

And we need to get there. Alive, preferably.

Sadie, who almost never surrendered the wheel of her beloved Jeep, seemed to understand and moved to the back seat.

Meanwhile, Liz tried to gain control of her thoughts, which had yelled and chased each other in her head like a courtroom of unruly lawyers. Perhaps if she could make them sit down and behave, she could understand what they were saying.

Liz first reviewed what they'd said about French as a possible kidnapper and about Mrs. Cross.

If French had kidnapped Jackson's mother, he must have been incredibly desperate or remarkably stupid.

Liz never would have voiced this to Jackson, but Mrs. Cross, with her saber-like tactics, would have made an excellent criminal. When it came to her son, that woman possessed a killer instinct.

Liz nipped that thought in the bud. Despite her dislike, she really shouldn't use such extreme terms, even in her thoughts. However, Jackson's mother had gone on the offensive when French served Jackson with the lawsuit. And like a lioness protecting her cub, she'd also pounced on Liz.

Wouldn't she then have tracked down the source of her son's current misery and attacked for all she was worth? Surely that would qualify as "important business," in her eyes. But why hadn't Mrs. Cross returned? What would keep her away from Jackson overnight?

Liz gulped. Had Therese somehow sniffed out something bigger than French's frivolous lawsuit? Seen something she wasn't supposed to see?

The implications slammed Liz so hard that for a few minutes, she could only stare out the window at the gray-and-white landscape fleeing past. They had just turned north onto Route 31, so less than an hour remained before they reached the antiques store. Should she upset Jackson with the possibilities?

Perhaps she needed to let her hypothesis simmer a bit before blurting it out. In the meantime, she should focus on something else. Liz wrenched her thoughts from Mrs. Cross to Toni and Jerusha—an odd couple in crime, if there ever was one.

If there was one. Liz bit her lip.

How had casual meetings at quilt shows led to a nasty partnership? Neither woman appeared the type to befriend strangers. According to Miriam, Jerusha couldn't even make friends within her own community, except for Amity.

Whether Jerusha and Toni had met at a quilt show or not, had someone else recruited them to work together? Perhaps French? Liz shook her head. His less-than-charming approach might work with Toni, but Liz couldn't imagine Jerusha caving to some English bully. Once again, Liz relived that moment in the jail when Jerusha's gaze singed her like iron from a smithy's fire.

"Gött knows," she'd said, when Liz questioned her. It was the look of a woman with a clean conscience.

However, Toni, in confessing, had implicated Jerusha. Houghton had found the stolen quilts in Jerusha's room. Firm evidence, tied up with a bow, nice and neat.

Perhaps too neat.

Liz hadn't considered the possibility that Toni had planted them there to frame Jerusha. Perhaps she could have done so if she had indeed attended Verena's wake that day when Liz had attempted to follow her. But how could Toni have gained access to Jerusha's room? Only the family would have gone upstairs.

Something about the whole scenario seemed wrong. Liz had seen Toni and Jerusha talking at the grocery store, but she'd sensed no real connection between them, certainly not the common purpose needed to steal, then fence quilts.

What if Jerusha was indeed innocent, and someone else had stolen the quilts and planted them in her bedroom? Perhaps her brother? But Hiram had sided with his sister against his wife. Certainly he would not have tried to incriminate Jerusha.

Liz recalled the visitation again, when so many people had come and gone. Perhaps the thief was a member of the Amish community.

Out-of-town relatives might have visited. Liz made a note to ask Miriam, who would know. Though how would an out-of-towner obtain quilts stolen in the Pleasant Creek area?

Besides, Liz mused, the staircase opened into the living room. No one could have gone upstairs to Jerusha's bedroom without being seen. Who would or could take that kind of a risk?

Only someone who could come and go, who fit so well into the background that no one would question his presence—

Liz didn't realize she'd gasped aloud.

"Are you all right?"

Jackson's voice startled her like a flashlight in the dark cave of her thoughts. "Uh—well—"

"You're not." His sideways glance searched her. "You're shivering. Should I turn up the heat?"

"No, no. I—"

"Tell us what you're thinking," Sadie ordered.

Liz couldn't. She needed to think more on it, before she gave voice to her thoughts. But she did voice her fears about the possibility of Mrs. Cross's confronting French, blundering into a corrupt operation much bigger than she expected.

"I'd thought of that too."

Jaw set, he said, "Sadie, we may need your protection more than we anticipated."

She patted her shotgun. "You got it."

"Something else on your mind, Liz?" As usual, he'd read her too well. She hesitated. "Yes. But I can't talk about it yet."

He nodded. "Tell us soon, okay? Don't try to handle it alone."

"Remember, we Material Girls share stuff," Sadie chimed in. "And you can tell Jackson too. He's kind of an honorary Girl."

Jackson's taut face relaxed in a grin. "Uh, thanks. I think."

Bless you, Sadie. You always make us smile. Liz also felt herself relax. She hadn't realized she'd been gritting her teeth.

They passed the Rochester exit and were nearing French's antique store.

"There it is." Sadie grasped her gun.

A vintage-style sign that read, *Yesteryear's Treasures* marked the small, slightly shabby business huddled between an insurance agency and a fast-food restaurant. No cars sat in the icy gravel parking lot in front of it. Unlike the other businesses, the store's front sidewalk was unshoveled. Jackson drove around the back. They saw two cars behind the insurance agency, and despite it being well past lunch hour, the blacktop parking lot of the fast-food restaurant held a number of cars. There was no sign of French's van, however. Snow had accumulated behind the antique store, and the building appeared deserted.

Had they come all this way for nothing?

Liz and Jackson vetoed Sadie's idea of accompanying them to the door carrying a gun, but they agreed that once parked by the front entrance, she could surreptitiously cover them as they knocked.

There was no answer. They peered through the windows into the cluttered shop and saw that the lights were off and no one seemed to be in there.

They drove around to the back door again. Liz and Jackson knocked again, but received the same lack of response.

Sadie joined them. "Maybe we should break in."

Thanks, Sadie, but I don't want to be thrown in jail. Liz patted Jackson's arm. "I know this is hard for you. I think we should call the local sheriff. First, though, let's ask the neighbors if they've seen French lately."

Jackson agreed, and Sadie deferred to his wishes, thank goodness.

Liz hesitated. "Sadie, we don't want to attract undue attention. Would you mind leaving your hat in the car?"

Sadie grumbled, but sans hat and shotgun, she accompanied Liz to the fast-food place, where she ordered a triple cheeseburger and large fries.

Liz contented herself—sort of—with a diet lemonade.

Sitting and sipping as Sadie devoured her wonderfully fragrant meal, Liz evaluated the employees. The cranky, no-nonsense assistant manager didn't appear very approachable. Ditto for the tight-mouthed older man at the cash register, who looked as if he'd rather be anywhere but there. She couldn't see the person working the drive-through. The teen girl at the counter looked bright-eyed and capable, but she was stealthily texting on her phone. Would she have looked up long enough to spot French going into his store?

Did she even know there was an antiques store next door?

Liz sighed, then stiffened.

A boy mopping floors near them might be the answer to her prayers. She read the name on his ID badge and added a little extra to her smile. "Hey, Ricky, I wonder if you could help me."

He paused and shot her a bored, "oh great" glance—which suddenly got more professional under Sadie's sharp look. "Uh, well, yeah, I guess I could try."

"My friend and I heard the guy next door sells wonderful antiques at great prices, but no one seems to be home." She added a note of pathos to her voice. "We've come a long way too."

"Miles and miles," Sadie added. "We have to see him!"

The young man nodded. "Mr. French has been closed all week, which is weird, even for this time of year. Maybe he's at his place over in Wabash."

"In Wabash?" Liz poured every scrap of charm she could summon into her smile.

"Yeah, Mr. French told me that this little store here is nothin'. He's got one of those storage places in Wabash, ya know? Filled it with special stuff he sells to rich people—and the IRS doesn't know diddly about it."

I'll bet the police don't know about this "special stuff" either. Liz said to Sadie, "Maybe we should go to Wabash. Mr. French must have a big selection there."

Ricky stirred uneasily. "You're not from the IRS, are you?"

"Watch your language," Sadie drawled, grinning as she shot a straw paper at him. "I hate paying taxes. Why would I work for those guys?"

A grin surfaced on Ricky's face. Liz thanked him, and he turned away to mop floors on the other side of the dining area.

Once outside, Liz said, "Well, French might think twice next time before boasting about his secret stash of goods." She tapped her cheek with an exaggerated gesture. "I wonder why they're *such* a secret."

"He bragged to a kid who works at Burger Heaven, no less." Sadie rolled her eyes. "The guy must have an ego like a Macy's parade balloon—and a brain filled with the same stuff."

"He apparently possesses enough brains to run a profitable if not necessarily legal business." Sadie and Liz opened the Jeep's doors and Liz took Sadie's keys to start the engine and heater from the passenger seat. "I'm going to try to track down this storage place on my phone. A shame we don't have an address, but Wabash isn't big. Surely there aren't many storage buildings in the area."

Sadie had plopped into the back seat. "Maybe Jackson had some luck at the insurance place."

He had. Using his mayoral charm and credentials, he'd wheedled the secretary into letting him see the boss, Patrick Bristol. Jackson apparently had impressed him as well. The garrulous agent talked freely about his old friend and his "deals," confirming that he hadn't seen him at the store for almost a week. "He told me French comes and goes as he pleases. Lucky guy."

Jackson told them how he had complimented Bristol on the quilted wall hanging in his office, with its muted colors and distinctive geometric shapes. "Is that Amish?" he'd asked.

"Yeah. As a matter of fact, French sold it to my wife." Bristol had shaken his head with a wry grin. Turned out, they'd visited his storage place near Wabash, "and she fell in love with it—and bought it for *my* birthday."

Jackson had wrangled directions from Bristol, though the agent cautioned, in a conspiratorial whisper, "Not sure French wants a lot of company there. You might call ahead of time and tell him what you want. Maybe he'll bring it here for you if you can stick around."

Jackson had deadpanned, "I hate to be rude, but we really were planning on surprising Mr. French."

Though Sadie and Liz had chuckled at this, their light mood evaporated as they drove toward Wabash.

About forty-five minutes later, on the town's outskirts, they spotted a line of run-down storage units and a small, nearby pole barn.

Liz tensed like a loaded spring.

Perhaps they should have called Chief Houghton after all.

16

Jackson turned onto the street beside the buildings, then took a left at the next street.

Liz spotted French's van and pointed.

Jackson inhaled. "That's his, all right."

Jackson parked in a small church's lot a little farther down the road. The scene was so peaceful, with snowflakes softly falling. Liz felt as if their little group had stepped into a Christmas card.

If only they could stay here forever. Liz sighed and turned to the others. "Okay. How are we going to do this?"

"I'd love to charge in and knock French through the wall." Sadie's eyes glinted. "But that's probably not the right approach."

"Any hint of my presence will make him run," Jackson added.

Liz said, "I don't know if he remembers me or not. French saw me at the town hall after your blowup, but that's the only incident that involved the two of us."

"The only one you know of, anyway." Jackson's gaze met hers, and Liz suppressed a shiver. The poisoned cupcake on her porch. The popcorn incident. Perhaps French's slime had seeped into her life more than she'd realized.

Sadie offered, "I could play 'dumb old lady.' But who would handle the protection part of things?"

"I can do that."

At Jackson's tone, Liz looked him in the eye. "I don't think that's a good idea, especially since we're far from sure that French played a major role in your mother's disappearance."

"She's right, Jackson," Sadie agreed. "What if we're way out in left field? Poppin' off without a gun is one thing. Poppin' off while aiming one might turn into something you'll regret. I'll talk to French. He doesn't know me."

Liz's stomach lurched at the thought of handling Sadie's shotgun, but she offered, "I've practiced with that thing, you know. I'll cover Sadie."

She wasn't used to Jackson's frown, dark as a blizzard cloud.

He finally said, "All right. But I'm not going to just sit and watch."

"Of course you won't," Liz assured him. "Let's figure out a plan." After they did so, Jackson drove the Jeep back to French's storage place and parked it along the street across from his van.

There was no way to hide the vehicle's hot-pink presence, but Liz, in her role of protector, would have to see and hear what went on. She prayed French didn't look out his pole barn's back windows.

Jackson zipped his coat and pulled on his ski mask. As always, Liz wondered at how those things could disguise wearers so completely.

A silent bell dinged in her mind, faint but definite as a phone's reminder. Ski masks were somehow important. Why? Liz bookmarked the thought for later.

Jackson touched Liz's hand, and her heart dropped as she thought of the danger they faced.

"See you in a little while," was all he said.

She couldn't have endured much more than that bare-bones goodbye.

Jackson opened the Jeep's door and tramped into the onslaught of powdery snow, egged on by a suddenly fierce wind.

Sadie donned her skunk hat again. "Wish I could carry my gun."

"You'll still be skunk-hunting," Liz said, "just using a different approach."

Sadie retrieved the shotgun from the back and handed it to Liz.

Her shoulder muscles complained. "Wow, I forgot how heavy this thing is."

"Prop the tip of the barrel on the windowsill," Sadie advised, "so you'll be ready to shoot if need be."

Liz nodded, her heart thudding against her ribs. She pulled up her hood to disguise her appearance and followed Sadie's directions, keeping the safety on and her finger off the trigger.

Liz turned to her friend, still standing by the open door. "I may not be able to see or hear everything from here. Signal me if he gets out of hand."

"I'll yank on my hat's tail." Sadie crossed the street, then meandered toward the building, slowing with each step. She ambled past the front of the van, peering into its only windows. Sadie jiggled the locked door and wagged her head a little, as if confused, and Liz knew she'd seen no clues from that limited perspective.

Sadie hadn't even made it to the pole barn's back door when it flew open and French, carrying two boxes, nearly ran her down.

"Young man," she squawked, loud enough to be heard down the block, "did your mama not teach you any manners?"

Sadie poked a finger in his face. "I heard you got them smiley-face rugs from the '60s here. I been looking all over Indiana, and I want to see 'em right now."

"Ma'am, this isn't a store. I rent storage units." French scowled as he retrieved the boxes he'd dropped.

She cut off his path to the van and yelled, "You're just tryin' to get rid of me, but I know all about what you do."

He halted for a split second, then used his boxes to shove her aside. "Get lost, you crazy old bat. I don't know anything about any smiley-face rugs."

"You do too," Sadie howled and swung her sizable purse at French's head.

Momentarily stunned, he recovered quickly and turned to slam into her again. Liz's hands tightened on the gun, but Jackson raced from the side of the nearest storage unit and knocked French flat with one punch.

As he jumped onto the man, Liz threw the car door open, slid the gun free, and hurried across the street. Sadie grabbed it and trained it on French's head. "One false move, mister, and you're a sausage patty."

He'd spouted obscenities at Jackson, but now, looking down the barrel of Sadie's gun, French's face collapsed in fear.

Jackson growled, "What did you do with my mother?"

The man muttered, "I don't know what you're talking about."

"We think you do." Liz glared at him. "She came to see you to discuss the lawsuit you filed against Jackson. Where is she? In a storage unit? In your van?"

French stared glumly past them.

"Maybe when we call the police, you'll feel more talkative." Jackson trussed French's wrists with duct tape he'd brought from Sadie's Jeep, then dug into their prisoner's pockets. Jackson found two sets of keys. Examining the smaller ring, he said, "This one looks like a door key—to the pole barn, I'll bet. The other is probably the key to the van. Let's search there first, then try this other ring of keys on the storage units."

"Meanwhile, I'll keep Mr. French company." Under the skunk face, Sadie's enormous smile spread across her face. "If you don't think I can shoot, just ask the coyotes that try to raid my chicken house."

Apparently the prospect of being left with Sadie frightened the man more than Jackson's punches. "I didn't do anything with your mom," French whined. "I didn't do anything *to* your mom. *She* took her away—"

Jackson froze. "She who?"

"Amity," Liz, suddenly sure, answered before French could. "Amity Bassinger."

The man nodded vehemently. Jackson's jaw dropped. Sadie nearly dropped her gun. She recovered quickly, though, aiming it even closer to French's head.

"I'll explain later." Liz turned back to French. "Where did Amity take Mrs. Cross?"

French babbled, "To an old barn on her farm. Not the one her dad uses. The one way out in the woods, off Muddy River Road."

"I assume Amity didn't drive her buggy," Liz said drily.

He snorted. "She keeps a four-wheel-drive truck here. I asked her not to leave it on my property, but she does anyway."

"Did Amity tell you anything else?" *Like what she plans to do with Mrs. Cross?*

"Nothing. I swear." Sweat broke out on French's face. "I told Amity not to hurt her. That your mom didn't know anything. Honest."

"We need to go." Jackson hauled French to his feet "Let's finish tying him up and leave him here."

"We can always call the Wabash police on the way and have them rescue him," Liz agreed, "though maybe after we find your mother might be best." If they didn't collect major evidence of French's part in all this, his current lawsuit against Jackson would seem like a Sunday school picnic compared to what he could do now. Liz, Jackson, and Sadie might very well face criminal charges for battery or confinement.

Liz brushed away such thoughts as they quickly duct-taped his ankles, stuck a strip across his mouth, and left him in his heated barn. French didn't protest. His eyes, following their exit, seemed even grateful, perhaps because they weren't leaving Sadie with him.

This time, Sadie was in the driver's seat, expertly operating the Jeep as if demons chased them. Liz, praying law enforcement wouldn't pull them over—and that they'd survive this ride—suggested Jackson call Chief Houghton. "He's more likely to believe you, I think."

Jackson didn't crack a smile. "Will do."

However, service in that area seemed nonexistent. Liz tried unsuccessfully too.

Desperately hoping they'd find his mother in time, she reached back and patted Jackson's hand. Liz could almost feel anxiety coursing through his veins.

Jackson's glance expressed his gratitude, but he seemed to have enclosed himself in an invisible shell.

Near their county line, Jackson finally got through to the chief. In terse sentences, he summarized Mrs. Cross's abduction by Amity and their encounter with French.

"A pileup? How long?" Jackson asked.

After he'd hung up, he leaned against the back of the seat. "The chief and all his officers are stuck out on the interstate with a real mess, including two fatalities. He says he'll free up an officer within fifteen minutes and ask the sheriff if he can send someone too." Jackson closed his eyes and gripped his head with both hands.

Over the Jeep's roar, Liz heard him say, "If only . . ."

She knew the finish of his sentence. If only he and his mother hadn't fought with each other throughout this visit. Throughout their entire lives.

Sadie's Jeep lurched from the highway onto Muddy River Road. They strained to see through clouds of snow.

Sadie squinted. "Should be coming to it soon."

Liz pointed to a half-covered gravel road. "Is that it?"

In answer, Sadie turned the Jeep onto the road, which took them through gloomy, bare-limbed woods. Liz glanced back at Jackson. Leaning as far forward as his seat belt allowed, he stared unblinking at the forest before them.

Finally, Jackson stabbed a finger to the left. "There's the barn."

They could see only a part of its tall roof from there, but Sadie steered the Jeep and trailer to the side of the road and stopped. They slipped in among the trees where the underbrush was thickest, flattening themselves against big trees, snowy rises, and dips in the terrain.

Now they could see the back of the enormous old building, certainly dilapidated as French had said, and leaning crazily to one side. Liz saw a truck parked inside, but no sign of life through the barn's cracked windows. However, dancing shadows cast by wind-blown branches easily could have camouflaged any movement.

Jackson silently gestured toward the opposite side of the barn—he would circle around in that direction. Liz and an armed Sadie crept along the splintery wall, stopping every few seconds to listen.

A woman's voice muttered angrily. Liz edged her nose past the corner, then spotted Amity.

The scene fixed in Liz's mind like a picturesque old snapshot—the Amish woman in black dress and shawl against the snow, hitching a horse team to a sleigh.

Jackson charged in from the other side of the barn. Liz and Sadie sprinted in as well.

Amity gave up on hitching up the horse and vaulted onto its back instead. She charged away.

"I'll get the Jeep!" Sadie dashed back toward her vehicle.

Jackson reached the sleigh first, yanked off blankets in the back, and clasped a large, tarp-covered bundle to his chest. He pulled away the tarp and hugged his mother tightly, then pulled out a pocketknife to cut through the ropes that bound her.

Sadie zoomed up in the Jeep, got out, and hustled to the trailer. "This thing'll go anywhere, but the snowmobile's faster, especially if we hit deep snow."

"So let's take it." Liz turned to Jackson. "Stay with your mother."

She scurried to help Sadie unload the snowmobile. She donned her helmet and jumped on the back, ignoring her mind's replay of her last ride. Sadie handed her the gun, and Liz made sure the safety was on.

The snowmobile roared to life and raced after its prey.

Sadie yelled over her shoulder, "I'm guessing Amity will follow this road to the end, probably to a field."

"We'll get her," Liz shouted. Grimly, she commanded her tired body to cling to Sadie and the shotgun. Participating in a real chase scene was not nearly as much fun as watching one at the movies.

The deep, powdery drifts must have impeded Amity's progress, because Sadie's snowmobile caught up with her as her horse charged out of the forest into the endless sea of snowy cornfields. The sun, dropping close to the western horizon, bathed the white land with blood-red light and wicked shadows. Amity's black hair had escaped its bonds, streaming behind her as she rode. As she flew across the landscape, she resembled an angel more than ever—just not the kind Liz had originally thought her to be.

"This is her farm. She must know it like the back of her hand," Liz shouted. She leaned forward, not wanting to blink, lest she lose sight of Amity. "She'll try to stop us dead in our tracks. Or confuse us."

Sadie called over her shoulder, "She doesn't know me. Or my ride."

She made Bunny's driving seem like a sweet little old lady's. However, Amity led them to a barbed-wire fence with a gate she had chained shut. Her horse jumped it easily.

Sadie stopped then threw the snowmobile into reverse. "Hang on."

Liz closed her eyes as her unstoppable friend rammed the snowmobile into the gate. *Wham!*

Liz's teeth banged together.

She opened her eyes. They'd only dented the metal gate, constructed to deter wayward cows.

"Let's do it again." Sadie backed the snowmobile farther.

Liz rubbed her aching jaws. "The fence doesn't look as strong. Shouldn't we try it instead?"

"With all that barbed wire? No, we'll make it this time." Sadie revved the motor and hunkered down.

Praying under her breath, Liz did the same.

A *whoosh* of freezing air. A crash that loosened her every ligament. Sadie crowed as they burst into the adjoining field. "Made it!"

Amazingly, the battered snowmobile zoomed over the next rise. Raising her eyes, Liz saw—

No one.

No horse, no rider in any direction.

With the land's small hollows and rises, Amity occasionally had disappeared for a few seconds during their chase, but she didn't reappear this time.

"She's gotta be around here somewhere," Sadie yelled.

Liz strained her eyes to follow the horse's snowy footprints in the snowmobile's headlights. However, the light reflecting off the snow made them harder to see, not easier.

Sadie's solution was to speed up and race in random directions.

Liz grimaced. *We might not know where we're going, but we're making excellent time.* Frantically, she scanned the darkening landscape again—and had an idea.

"Sadie, go back to where we saw her last," Liz commanded. At Sadie's glare, she explained.

Her friend's scowl faded, and moments later they were within shouting distance of their last glimpse of Amity. As they neared it, a deep, narrow depression materialized in the land, filled with snowy, scraggly bushes.

"Wait a second, Sadie." The machine stopped and Liz called the chief and tried to describe where she thought they were.

Fortunately, he knew. "Clinton Creek. Used to play there when I was a kid. I'll send the boys that way." His voice changed. "Hey, wanted you to know I found Brett Landry, Crystal's no-show date. In Lexington. Confirmed Crystal's story. Also, shortly before the time of Verena's murder, he saw a woman and man who fit Amity's and French's descriptions at Jaynes Lake."

"Great work, chief," she said, grinning.

"Thanks," he replied drily. "Now, I've got a few boys heading out to where you are. Don't—"

Liz hung up before he could finish telling her not to pursue Amity, then nodded to Sadie.

Without hesitation, Sadie barreled the snowmobile into the creek bed's depths.

Instantly, the growing twilight enclosed them with murky shadows—shadows that could easily hide Amity and her horse. Liz didn't doubt she'd use whatever means possible to stop them. Her hand tightened on the shotgun, trying to steady it as the snowmobile lurched and skidded on the creek bed's icy floor.

They'd prowled perhaps a quarter mile when Sadie stiffened. "Something just moved ahead of us. Something big." Suddenly she yelled, "Shoot, Liz!"

She stared. "But what if—"

"Up into the air. Shoot straight up in the air!"

A hint of comprehension jabbed Liz's brain, and she took off the safety and aimed toward the first twinkling stars.

Bam!

The shotgun's force nearly knocked her off the snowmobile.

She grabbed Sadie as her friend floored it. Skeletal branches smashed against them as the vehicle lunged along the creek bed.

"Scared that horse to kingdom come," Sadie exulted as she guided their crazy path.

Sure enough, its headlights revealed a flash of tail and haunches about a hundred yards ahead of them.

The *crack* of a pistol shot also confirmed Amity's presence—and that she was also armed.

"Keep your head down!" Sadie shouted. "I'm going to run that critter out of this ditch!"

Instead, Liz steadied the shotgun as Sadie plunged madly ahead, pulling within perhaps thirty feet of Amity's horse. "If I let loose another shot, maybe that will do that trick."

"Give me seven seconds," Sadie said.

The snowmobile swerved forward, ducking bushes. When Liz caught a glimpse of Amity astride the horse, she aimed at the sky and squeezed the trigger again.

This time, Amity's horse hurled itself up the side of the ditch.

"Woo-hoooo!" Sadie bellowed as her valiant snowmobile scaled the wall.

"Yes!" Liz yelled triumphantly as they pushed over the top.

Amity's runaway horse already had galloped several hundred feet ahead. But pulsating blue-and-red lights greeted her from the roads surrounding the field. ATVs roared in from several directions, and Liz thought she would weep with joy when she heard the chief's voice over the loudspeaker. "Amity Bassinger, we have you surrounded. Give it up."

But Amity wasn't done. She tried to elude her pursuers by circling the horse to gallop in the opposite direction. Sadie charged after her, and a tall rider on a similar horse intercepted Amity. She pushed frantically at him as he grabbed her reins, but with one shove, he knocked her from the horse into a drift.

Liz jumped from the snowmobile even before Sadie could stop.

She pointed the shotgun at Amity, splayed in the soft snow. "Breathe the wrong way, and it will be your last." Amity didn't have to know that the safety was on.

Jackson leaped from the horse, which Liz recognized as the other from Amity's sleigh team. "You've always had a way with words, Liz. Couldn't have said it better myself. I'd better call Mom and let her know everything is all right." He took his phone from his pocket and called.

"How can you treat me this way?" Amity whined from the ground. "I have cared for the sick and dying."

Liz glared at her. "You care for no one but yourself. You turned sweet Toni into a criminal. You turned French, a little crook, into a murderer like yourself. You stole a mother from three little boys who believed you were their friend, and you stole another mother from her only son. You tried to kill me with a poisoned cupcake. Whatever good you have done, it doesn't hold a candle to the bad."

Amity laughed softly. "Are you so righteous, Liz? You who come between the man you seem to care for and his only family, his mother?"

"He stays for the love of his town," Liz said, realizing the truth of her words as she spoke them. "And for his dedication to protecting Pleasant Creek's citizens from people like you."

She glanced at Jackson, who had just hung up with his mother and was beaming at her.

An ATV pulled up beside Liz. Chief Houghton leveled his own weapon at Amity as he jumped out. "We'll take it from here, Liz."

Sadie took the shotgun from her, and Jackson threw his warm, safe arms around her.

It was all over.

17

On Sunday morning, Liz found herself walking to the jail again. After the apprehension of Amity, she'd called Rob Carver as promised and given him the scoop on what had happened.

Toni had asked that Liz visit her as soon as she could. Perhaps Toni couldn't handle looking into the faces of her Sisterhood friends and telling them she'd been involved in theft.

Toni's depression had increased during her stay at Liz's inn. This arrest and the bleak prospect of prison might prove more than she could endure. Perhaps a caring ear this morning could make a difference. Liz climbed the steps to the heavy glass doors and entered.

The dispatcher welcomed Liz with a quizzical look. "Back again? I would have thought the hours of visiting with Jerusha Suter the other night would have been enough."

More than enough. "Will Jerusha be released soon?"

"Probably tomorrow if the paperwork goes through."

"Good." Liz followed the officer back to the visitation area. Officer Hughes brought in Toni. Her white face, with black circles under leaden eyes, posed a stark contrast to her orange prison garb.

Had she slept at all last night? Liz doubted it.

Toni picked up the phone with a pleading look through the glass.

"Thanks for coming." Toni's chin dipped, and she studied the floor. "I know I don't deserve favors from you—or anybody else."

"I want to help if I can." Liz wished she could hug the fragile-looking woman. "You have to know, though, that I can't keep anything you tell me confidential. If it's relevant to this case, I have to inform the police."

"I know." A tear dribbled down her cheek, but she still didn't look up. "I can't believe I got myself into this mess. Why did I listen to Amity?"

"I imagine she's very persuasive. She fooled all of us into thinking she was a good person, with all of the help she gave the needy in her community, but she was a criminal the whole time."

"She was always warm and friendly at those quilt shows, so much nicer than Jerusha. I usually went alone, and she made me feel like I had a friend. And with all my troubles—personal, financial, all of it—I really needed a friend. When she proposed that we team up to sell Amish quilts, I thought she was the answer to my prayers."

So she hadn't known the quilts were stolen. *Poor Toni.*

"Over several months, I sold a number of quilts and believed we were on our way to a great partnership. Maybe I'd even get to keep my house." Her mouth trembled. "As time went on, though, Amity became more and more secretive about where the quilts were coming from, and that made me uneasy. Finally, I caught her in an outright lie. I decided to tell her I wanted out."

"No wonder you seemed upset when you came to the inn," Liz said gently.

Toni nodded, finally looking up at Liz. "Originally, I'd suggested that our group come to Pleasant Creek's FebFest so I could meet with Amity in my spare time and collaborate on expanding our business." Her hands clenched. "But she avoided me. I only found Amity's farm because Jerusha told me its location."

"When you saw each other in town that day?"

"Yes. I drove out to Amity's farm and confronted her."

"That was brave of you."

"My courage didn't last long," Toni said bitterly. "Amity laughed in my face. She admitted she'd stolen most of the quilts I'd sold, but if I stopped or breathed a word, she'd expose me as a coconspirator."

Ingenious, in a terrible way. What a nightmare.

"I didn't want to tell Amity that Sofia had seen the stolen quilt. I was terrified that she'd make good on her threats, as she'd slapped me around when I told her I wanted out. I was worried she'd go after Sofia. But I knew Amity would find out—it was like she had a spy cam on me all the time—and then she would kill me. So I told her."

Strange that the deceitful Amity had demanded honesty. "How did Amity react?" Liz asked.

"She was all sweetness and light." Toni shuddered. "I'm not sure which of her moods was worse. Amity told me she'd take care of things and that I should find an excuse to leave, but she wasn't helping me. She was covering her tracks."

Toni hadn't covered her own tracks very well. Liz probed, "Why did you bring that stolen quilt into your room? Sofia was bound to see it."

Toni picked at her uniform. "Stupidity, I guess. Maybe the dumbest thing I did."

"Maybe deep down, you wanted Sofia to find it."

"Probably. Yeah. I also knew that if I ran, I'd get caught." She stared at Liz with wide eyes. "I've never been in trouble before. Why didn't I just go to the police in the first place?"

Liz was furious. The fear of losing her house had driven unsuspecting Toni into the clutches of a predator.

Instead of sympathizing, though, Liz looked her in the eye. "So Amity 'took care of things' by planting two stolen quilts in Jerusha's room. And you accused her of masterminding the thefts."

Toni's pale cheeks flooded with shame. "When I was on the run, I called Amity. She said if I was caught, I should blame Jerusha for everything. I did what I was told." Toni covered her face with her hands. "I accused an innocent person. How could I do such a thing?"

Toni wept and wept, tears seeping through her hands and raining on her orange uniform.

Despite the woman's faults, Liz again wished she could hug her.

Finally, Toni's sobs quieted. "Do you think the courts will understand that I was afraid Amity would kill me?"

"I know the judges and prosecutors in this county are caring people of integrity," Liz answered. "You must tell them the whole truth. Offer any insights into Amity and her activities you can, but take responsibility for your own actions. Perhaps your lack of a record will minimize your sentence."

Toni nodded mutely.

Liz softened her voice. "Don't go through this alone, Toni. Let your friends help you."

The woman covered her face again. "They won't want anything to do with me."

"I think you're wrong. We all make mistakes," Liz coaxed. "They want to see you. So will my friends, the Material Girls. And I certainly do too."

Toni hesitated, then let her hands slide into her lap. "Thank you, Liz." No hint of a smile brightened her face, but the heaviness in her eyes had lightened. "I really do appreciate your coming today."

"I'm glad I did."

After saying goodbye, she hurried to church. Slipping into a back pew, Liz caught the last half of the sermon. After the service, she met up with Mary Ann and Sadie, who was now wearing a green-and-orange crocheted hat with huge purple flowers.

"Liz. You made it." Her friends enclosed her in their arms. Opal, Caitlyn, and Naomi joined them in forming one big nest of a hug.

Caitlyn felt Liz's head and shoulder in a quick exam. "Still in one piece? I wasn't sure you were."

"A little sore from those snowmobile rides, but overall I'm good."

As they laughed and kidded her, Liz wondered if blood sisters could be any closer.

Jackson stood to the side, but his face shone as he held out his arm. "May I escort you to the brunch the church ladies have so kindly prepared for us?"

"Brunch?" Before going to see Toni, Liz had hurriedly set up a continental breakfast for her sleeping guests with a note of explanation and promised partial refund to cover the usual full breakfast.

"They invited your guests too." Jackson winked. "Mary Ann's doing."

As she took his arm, Liz beamed her gratitude. "You're incredible friends. All you Girls are amazing."

"And I'm not?" Jackson protested in an injured tone.

"You are." She softened her voice. "In a one-of-a-kind way."

He halted as if stunned, but a million-dollar smile spread across his face.

Liz paused too, but not for the same reason.

During the hugs and banter, Mrs. Cross had approached. She looked poised and stylish—none the worse for her ordeal. The woman stood apart from the group, saying nothing.

There's a miracle.

Her keen gaze, however, had monitored every action and word.

"They invited Mom too." Jackson's pleading look touched first Liz, then Mrs. Cross.

Liz stepped toward his mother. "Please join us."

"Thank you." The woman's words sounded uncomfortable, as if she were unused to saying them.

Mary Ann immediately slipped to her side as the group made their way to the church's family center.

Chief Houghton and the Sisterhood met them in the foyer. The women exchanged hugs and explained that Chuck and Wayne were going over their snowmobiles one last time before the race and wouldn't be attending the brunch.

Bunny wore a silky royal-blue pantsuit and a crocheted rabbit-head hat.

"Sadie gave me the hat," was the unnecessary explanation. "I thought it would be perfect for today."

Somehow, it was.

Pastor Brad gave thanks for the meal, and what a meal! Liz couldn't imagine how her friends had cooked such a marvelous brunch on such short notice. There were quiches, casseroles, breakfast pizzas and enchiladas; a watermelon "basket" of fruit; and an array of homemade pastries, rolls, coffee cakes, and muffins unmatched by any Boston Sunday morning spread. This was a feast for the heart as well as the stomach, and healing for the terrors of the past two weeks.

"I wish Toni could have been here," she said to Bunny.

The tough woman's eyes moistened. "So do I." She glanced at Chief Houghton and his wife, talking with Jackson. "Do you think the chief would let me take her a plate when I visit later?"

"He might bend the rules this time." Liz smiled when the chief's nod confirmed her assurances. He'd clearly been listening in.

Caitlyn popped a last piece of cherry-cheese Danish into her mouth. "Well, what do you know? Crystal finally made it." The young nurse stood and hurried over to the skater just as she began a beeline toward Jackson. "I know you want to stay skinny," she told Crystal, grabbing her by the arm and dragging her toward the tables, "but you just *have* to try the chocolate-mint cream puffs."

Bless you, Caitlyn Ross. From the look on Jackson's face, he felt the same way.

Sitting beside him, she saw him do what she finally dared to do—cast occasional glances toward his mother.

How strange to exist in the same room with Mrs. Cross without wishing for a suit of armor.

Not that Jackson's mother had lapsed into a warm, fuzzy mode.

The woman still puckered her lips, even at the most delicious food. She gave Sadie's crocheted hat pained glances and did not bother to soften her frown at Bunny's.

Mary Ann, however, managed her well, as Caitlyn did Crystal. The skater planned to leave town immediately after her final performance, bragging that she'd talked the obliging Chuck and Wayne into carrying her considerable luggage to the car.

For once, Liz didn't mind her manipulative ways.

After eating, the Sunshine Sisterhood group left for FebFest because they were in the snowmobile race with Wayne and Chuck.

Liz and the others wished their new friends good luck. "Sorry we can't watch you compete, but we're committed to the Frozen Turkey Bowl," Liz said. Privately, she reflected that if she never saw another snowmobile again, it would be too soon.

"No problem," Bunny assured her while she loaded a plate of goodies for Toni. "Hope we can show you the first-place trophy before we go home."

"I'll be back at the inn for coffee hour," Liz promised.

Then she'd dress and go with Jackson to the Sweetheart Dance. When she glanced at him, Jackson's smile told her he was thinking the same thing.

Sadie obliterated the magic. "Well, I s'pose some of you want to know what really happened when we performed our duty as law-abiding citizens."

"You'd better tell us." Mary Ann leveled her gaze at Liz, Jackson, and Chief Houghton.

"Why don't you tell it, Liz?" the chief suggested. "I'll fill in whatever you leave out or don't know."

Liz took a deep breath and began.

18

Liz looked around the table at her closest friends—the Material Girls, Jackson, the chief—as well as at Crystal and Mrs. Cross. "Am I correct in saying Amity was the huge surprise?"

A hum of lingering amazement greeted her words.

Naomi shook her head. "When Mary Ann told us, I couldn't believe it. Even her name means 'friendship.' Amity seemed to epitomize it."

"You've *got* to be kidding." Caitlyn let both hands drop on the table. "It was like Mother Teresa had masterminded a con."

"Greed and a sense of power must have gotten to Amity," said Liz. "However, the original concept—recruiting Amish women to steal their friends' and families' quilts, then selling them at excellent prices—was Daryl French's. At least, according to him."

"We may not believe everything French tells us," Chief Houghton said wryly, "but we're already finding evidence in three other Amish communities that he'd employed women there as well."

"If you don't consider morals, it was a brilliant idea," Liz said. "Many Amish women are quilting experts and produce beautiful work. They circulate freely in each other's homes and entrust each other with their possessions. Best of all, they're members of highly virtuous communities, so no one would suspect them of participating in theft and burglary."

"Amity would be the last one anybody would suspect." Sadness filled Mary Ann's face. Sadie, sitting beside her friend, hugged her.

Mrs. Cross, however, sat like a marble statue.

Liz didn't blame her in the least, though she said, "Perhaps in her early years, Amity did care about others. She certainly kept her finger on the pulse of her community." Liz sighed. "Unfortunately, as you know, single Amish women aren't granted a significant status, no matter how kind or gifted. They're expected to spend their entire lives tending other women's families."

"That must have made her fiancé's betrayal even more difficult." Mary Ann shook her head. "Amity hid her bitterness very well for a while. But unresolved resentment can destroy a person."

"And did it ever," Sadie interjected.

Liz nodded. "French must have caught Amity at exactly the wrong moment, when she had grown weary of serving everyone else with little visible reward. Last night, along with the chief, I watched a video of the Wabash police interrogating French. He said he'd viewed Amity as the most promising of his Amish contacts and considered having her supervise a large portion of his operation. Amity, however, had her own ideas about who was in charge." Liz paused to stir cream into a cup of coffee.

The chief agreed. "When French warned Amity not to pull several thefts or burglaries in a row because it would attract too much attention, she ignored him. She stole other items as well as quilts, including cash and small Amish articles that could be sold in French's store or to other antique store owners for big profits."

Liz continued, "At first, French didn't try to rein her in because Amity was making him money, with the potential for a lot more. Eventually, though, he began to suspect she was keeping a large percentage of the cash herself. Instead of working under him, Amity was taking over. She began to threaten him the same way she threatened Toni."

"Did she have anything to do with Verena Suter's death?" Opal's mild blue gaze sharpened.

Liz exchanged looks with the chief. When he nodded, she said,

"I'm afraid so. When Amity realized Verena suspected her of stealing Hiram's cash and a relative's quilt, she decided Verena should be eliminated. When French protested, she convinced him that with Hiram's and Jerusha's attitudes toward Verena, the police would nab them as the murderers. She was very nearly right."

"If I'd had enough evidence to get a warrant to search Hiram's farm for the murder weapon, I'd have done it." Chief Houghton shook his head. "But motive and opportunity on their part and suspicion on mine wasn't quite enough."

"Fortunately, based on Toni's and French's confessions, the judge agreed to a search of Amity's farm," Liz said. "Her father's hammers and other heavy tools are now being tested for Verena's blood. Amity had figured the police would search the lake for her weapon, so she probably only rinsed it before taking it home. Hiding it in plain sight was an arrogant move. She must have thought no one would ever suspect her."

Caitlyn held up a hand. "So Amity was the one who actually killed Verena? Or did she talk French into doing it?"

"They're accusing each other," the chief answered, "so both are being charged with murder and conspiracy, as well as theft. However, I believe French when he says he didn't want to kill Verena. Amity threatened him into being the lookout and helping transport Verena to the shanty."

"French is a sneak and a thief," Liz agreed, "but he's not comfortable killing. Otherwise, he would have gotten rid of Amity when she started to take over."

"Let's hope some of these more specific tests help confirm the actual murderer before the trials start," the chief said. "I also found Brett Landry, who not only confirmed Crystal's alibi"—he nodded toward her—"but earlier this morning identified Amity and French as the people he saw on the lake path shortly before the time of the murder."

"I'm glad he could help." Crystal's lip still stuck out in a pout. "But the creep should have told me he was married!"

At least Landry had displayed enough conscience not to show up for their evening date. Flinching, Liz hoped Crystal wouldn't bring up anything more—

"But you believed I was like him. You thought I had something going with Hiram." Crystal glared at Liz and the chief. "News flash: I don't date married guys. Especially my friends' husbands. And especially guys like *Hiram*." She rolled her eyes.

"You thought she was dating Hiram Suter?" Caitlyn stared at Liz as if she'd lost her mind.

Liz and the chief had apologized abjectly, but it appeared more groveling was needed. "I'm so sorry to have embarrassed you, Crystal," Liz said, "but remember, you were seen together in Fort Wayne more than once."

"Hiram's got a good reputation as a builder, and he used to work construction for my dad," Crystal protested. "I just wanted him to help me with plans for my dream house when I retire from skating." She scowled at the others. "I was thinking of building it around Pleasant Creek. But maybe you all think that just because I'm a blonde, I'm *that* kind of woman?"

"I certainly made assumptions that weren't true," Liz said soothingly. "Will you forgive me?" She held out her hand.

The chief did likewise. "I really am looking forward to your performance this afternoon."

Crystal paused to prolong the drama, then condescended to take their hands. "I forgive you." She flashed a gracious smile, then swept the table with a bright, fluttery glance. "I hope you all come to see me skate before I leave. Sorry to eat and run, but I have practice."

As Liz expected, she glued her best smile to Jackson.

He stood and responded with his mayor's handshake. "Thank you so much for visiting our town. You've helped make it a special FebFest."

"Um, yeah." Crystal's shining smile waxed and waned like an uncertain moon. She turned and left.

A collective sigh of relief wafted through the room.

Liz blessed Sadie for changing the subject. "I'm still trying to figure out how Amity and French got Verena to the shanty. The weather was up and down that afternoon, but some people were around, skating and fishing. How did those scuzzballs keep from being seen?"

The chief's fist tapped the table. "Actually, they were seen. But nobody caught on, including me, until Liz figured it out."

"The whole scenario was Amity's idea, of course." How Liz wished the woman had devoted her superior brain to other endeavors. "I'd figured that two people were involved, but I originally thought a driver helped carry the body up to a car, then took it to the shanty.

"Because Jerusha told her about Verena's 'deserting' the family to go skating, Amity knew ahead of time the approximate time and location where she and Crystal would meet. Amity saw immediately that she would need a partner, so she bullied French until he agreed to help her."

"What a wimp." Sadie's nose wrinkled as if he belonged to a new species of slug.

Liz went on, "French made some preparations before the murder. First, he widened the hole in the ice inside the fishing shanty so they could hide Verena's body. Then he sawed part of a log from one of the big decomposing trees left from the floods a few years ago. When Sadie and I examined the crime scene, we saw that piece of sawn log not far from the shanty, but I didn't figure out its significance in the crime until later."

Mary Ann prompted, "And that was?"

"Amity and French used it to transport Verena over the ice to the shanty," Liz said. "I think it went something like this: Amity, wearing a ski mask and a dark snowsuit so blood wouldn't show, assaulted Verena. Then she and French carried the log section to the crime scene. Verena was small and thin, so they had no trouble fitting her inside. They put a ski mask on Verena and tucked a blanket around her. French helped Amity carry the log to the ice. She shoved it along, talking and laughing. The witnesses the chief interviewed said they saw a couple of kids playing on the ice at the time of the murder, but no one else."

A murmur of shock and disgust ran through the group.

"Laughing? The woman was *laughing* right after she murdered someone?" Opal's eyes hardened into blue ice. "I can't believe a human being would do that."

Caitlyn shuddered. "She makes me feel like taking a bath."

"Two baths," Mary Ann agreed, "but what made you put all that together, Liz?"

"Actually, the sled wasn't the first clue that helped me think this through," she answered. "For some reason, ski masks stood out in my mind. When we skated before discovering Verena's body, when we went snowmobiling, and when Jackson donned a ski mask before we captured French—they all struck me as excellent disguises. Had Verena's killers worn them? As I continued to puzzle about how the partners transported the body to the shanty, I wondered if they disguised *Verena* with a ski mask, in case someone saw them after the murder. But that would only work in the context of pretending to take her to the hospital after injury—which would attract all kinds of attention—or in the context of a winter sport. Sledding fit the bill perfectly, especially as Sadie had remarked about kids using rotten logs as sleds. Then I realized that after the killing, Amity and French hid their 'sled' as a natural part of the landscape—again, in plain sight."

Jackson whistled. "Did you figure this out while we were riding to Amity's farm?"

"Some of it. By the time I talked to the chief after she was arrested, I'd realized a ski mask could have held a towel or bandage in place, stanching blood, eliminating a blood trail from the crime scene to and inside the shanty. It also could have accounted for Verena's badly disheveled hair and Kapp."

"Liz suggested that crime dogs sniff around Amity's farm," the chief went on. "I got a call after church this morning. The blood on ski masks, gloves, snowsuit, and towel the dogs found buried in Clinton Creek, was Verena's. I also wouldn't be surprised if we find Amity's hair on that stuff—more material for DNA testing."

Exclamations filled the air:

"Whoa, Liz!"

"You go, girl!"

"You're amazing!"

"Way to go, Sherlock!"

Naomi's eyes, however, still blazed like twin torches. "Who tried to kill Liz with that cupcake?"

Chief Houghton spoke again. "French confirmed that Amity baked it."

Liz nodded. "Everyone knows she's an excellent baker. I saw a gorgeous chocolate cake at Verena's wake. Its frosting resembled the professional-looking frosting on that cupcake. I didn't make the connection at the time, but I'll bet she made both."

"French paid a loafer from Wildton to deliver it," the chief continued. "I talked to the guy, and French had told him it was a Valentine's Day surprise for his girl." Houghton snorted. "French also claimed that Amity deceived him. She told him she just wanted to scare Liz off, that she'd only mixed in enough arsenic to make Liz sick."

Mary Ann scoffed, "She'd kill Verena, but show 'mercy' to Liz? I don't think so."

Houghton said, "French did, however, admit to the popcorn episode."

"Popcorn?" His listeners, except for Naomi and Jackson, stared.

Liz smiled and shrugged. "I guess I didn't tell you other Girls about that."

Naomi explained.

"Um, that's creepy," Caitlyn said.

Naomi scooted closer to Liz and hugged her. "Those people are downright pathological."

Liz tried to smile. "Yes, they probably could use some therapy."

It might be awhile before she ate cupcakes or popcorn again.

"You poor thing," Opal said, touching Liz's hand.

"My troubles are nothing compared to what the Suters have suffered. And how much more those little boys will suffer with Amity's betrayal." Liz's eyes filled with tears.

Sadie's did too, but hers were tears of rage. "I'm glad we went out and captured that scum!" She blew her nose, a sound which reverberated like a foghorn, interrupting the group's sadness and making everyone smile.

Liz turned to Mrs. Cross, who had said little throughout the talk. "We're all thankful you're with your son, safe and sound."

Mrs. Cross's eyes widened.

The chief said quickly, "Good thing you rescued her when you did. Amity had told her father she was going to help their sick Ohio relatives for a day or two. However, French said that once Amity put some distance between her and Pleasant Creek, she planned to kill Mrs. Cross and dump her in a reservoir on the way."

Jackson hugged his mother.

She held her cheek against his, then said drily, "If ever I was in the wrong place at the wrong time, that was it. I overheard those two arguing about stolen merchandise and money and leaving the country. I told them, 'I know all about people like you.'"

"Amity apparently thought you knew much more than you did," Jackson said. "She wasn't terribly rational at that point, I guess."

Sadie aimed a thumb at the exit. "Are we done with this stuff? Because I'm due to win the Frozen Turkey Bowl in a half hour."

"You mean you're due to take second to me," Caitlyn taunted her.

"That's what you think," Jackson said. "This is my year."

"Frozen Turkey Bowl?" Mrs. Cross stared at her son.

Everyone laughed and hurried toward the door, but Mrs. Cross hung back and gestured to Liz to do the same.

Liz looked at her curiously.

"Thank you," Mrs. Cross said in the same tone she might have used in giving a phone number.

"You're welcome."

Mrs. Cross nodded and went to catch up with Mary Ann. Liz resumed kidding Caitlyn and Sadie about their competition. With one ear, though, she caught Mrs. Cross's aside to Mary Ann, "Perhaps I was a little hasty in my earlier opinions. Liz *is* an intelligent woman, and quite capable . . ."

Then Mrs. Cross lowered her voice so Liz couldn't hear the rest of her comments, but that fragment warmed her like the very best hot chocolate.

She—and everyone else—did hear Mrs. Cross, loud and clear, when she announced, "I am *not* going to the Turkey Bowl, whatever that is."

"Oh, but you really don't want to miss it, Therese." Mary Ann swept the woman out the door before she knew what was happening.

Liz, watching with Jackson through the family center's glass doors, saw Sadie practically stuff Mrs. Cross into her Jeep.

"You know your mother's in for the ride of her life, don't you?" Liz grinned as Sadie peeled out.

Jackson didn't answer in words.

But he laughed all the way to his car.

19

"How can I cheer for just one of our friends?" Liz asked as she and Naomi surveyed the icy Turkey Bowl lane.

"You don't have to." Naomi unrolled a white vinyl banner. "Hold onto your end, please."

Liz helped unfurl and raise the banner. Its big red letters proclaimed, *Good luck, Caitlyn, Jackson, and Sadie!*

Other bundled-up spectators brandished similar banners and sported boas, turkey headdresses, and elaborate feathered tails in honor of their favorites.

Dancing for numerous cameras and phones aimed at her, Sadie yelled, "Time for the annual 'Turkey Bowl Cheer'!"

The burgeoning audience roared their approval, then yelled with her:

Hit those pins, don't you bobble,

Make a strike, and we'll all gobble!

Then, flapping "wings," they all shrieked their best turkey imitations:

Gobble, gobble, gobble, go!

"They must have instituted this little custom after I left town." Mrs. Cross looked as frozen as the expired turkeys that were lined up for the event.

"We did," Mary Ann answered cheerfully, smoothing the feathery boa that matched the one Sadie wore. "This started about ten years ago. A shame we didn't think of it before."

Mrs. Cross's mouth wobbled, but no words came out.

Remembering Sadie's past efforts with both real bowling balls and turkeys, though not at the same time, Liz breathed a silent prayer. *Please let this go well. With no injuries to Sadie or anyone else.*

Sadie pranced to the line, wound up like a pro baseball pitcher, and hurled the turkey. It stayed airborne so long, Liz feared it would miss the pins entirely.

Instead, the turkey dropped in front of them and wiped out every pin.

"*Steee-rike!*" Sadie slung her boa in circles above her head.

The crowd gobbled and cheered.

Mrs. Cross touched her gloved hand to her forehead.

A few bowlers later, Caitlyn took her turn. As her hospital buddies hoisted a papier mâché turkey wearing a nurse's hat and stethoscope, Caitlyn displayed beautiful bowling form, also making a strike.

Soon Jackson, cheered by many townspeople, as well as numerous Amish supporters, readied his turkey.

Suddenly there was a screech that could be heard on the other side of Jaynes Lake. "*Go, Jackson! You can do it!*"

Lowering his turkey, he stared at his mother, along with everyone else who'd met formidable, refined Mrs. Cross.

The crowd snickered. His face reddened like a teenager's, but a tiny grin crept across his face as Jackson strode forward and sent all the pins flying.

"That's my boy!" roared Mrs. Cross.

All three of Liz's friends stayed neck and neck throughout the contest. By the last frame, Sadie and Caitlyn were duking it out for second place, with Jackson on top by five pins.

"You're going down, Ross!" Sadie threatened. "You too, Mayor!"

Sadie's windup this time would make highlight reels. However, the bird took its revenge by slipping from her grip. A universal "Ooh!" sounded from the crowd as Sadie sent it flying into a neighboring parking lot, where the turkey *whomped* a Chevy pickup's grill.

The crowd roared with laughter until the judge threatened to disqualify Sadie.

After a loud and extensive debate between Sadie, the judge, and the crowd, the judge finally shrugged. "Well, okay. No disqualification. But I sure would like to see sensible rules in place by the next FebFest."

Rational rules for the Frozen Turkey Bowl? "Yeah, right," Liz whispered to Naomi.

Besides, defined rules would eliminate Sadie from every contest, and nobody wanted that—even the owner of the Chevy pickup.

Jackson finally won, and Mrs. Cross beat Liz and the rest of the crowd in bursting from the sidelines to congratulate him.

Liz stepped back so they could share this crazy, loving moment, but Jackson pulled her close. "Can't wait for this evening," he whispered in her ear.

She caught her breath. Thank goodness for the chilly air that cooled her heated cheeks.

Jackson shouted to his constituents, "Since I won this, does that make me a first-class turkey?"

Amid laughter, he accepted his tacky plastic-and-metal turkey trophy.

"I guess I don't feel so bad losing to our honorary Material Girl," Sadie admitted, punching Jackson in the arm. "But look out next time!"

"Ditto." Caitlyn laughed. "I'll destroy you two!"

Afterward, Liz considered absenting herself from Crystal's final performance. She'd endured one—didn't that suffice? What grand finale would she employ for this one? From the fading smile and slight droop of Jackson's shoulders, she knew his thoughts matched hers. With his mother clasping his arm, though, he walked manfully toward the skating rink, obviously resolved to finish his mayoral duties.

"Girls, let's all go watch Crystal," Sadie proposed. "If she tries anything with Jackson, we'll charge onto the ice and tackle her."

Liz immediately felt better. "Oh, that would look great on an Internet video. We'd go viral."

"Liz, you of all people shouldn't let her get away with stuff." Sadie dragged her along as the other Girls followed, grinning. "Are you a woman, or are you a mouse?"

Liz really did want to see Crystal perform. Plus, though she wouldn't admit it to Sadie, she couldn't bear the thought of the skater getting away with more "stuff." But what could she do that wouldn't embarrass Jackson to death and keep the Pleasant Creek grapevine gabbling for the next hundred years?

Liz was still debating as she watched Crystal skate as only a champion could. Jumps, turns, and spins, with exquisite footwork and expressive, graceful arm movements left the crowd—and Liz—breathless.

After the skater bowed to signal the end of her routine, Liz could only watch as Crystal, smile glittering more than her skintight costume, skated toward Jackson.

He brought his mother, her arms full of roses, out from the stands and spoke into a microphone. "I'm delighted to have my mother here to congratulate our featured skater, Ms. Crystal Starling."

Crystal stared blankly as Mrs. Cross's elegant, controlled voice sounded over the PA system. "Thank you, my dear. We shall never forget that spectacular performance."

Mrs. Cross placed the bouquet in Crystal's arms while Jackson took the mic. Several steps away, he congratulated the skater. Mrs. Cross beckoned to photographers and posed with the confused young woman while Jackson, on the other side of his mother, smiled for several pictures. While the photo session continued, he edged off the ice and hurried to Liz's side.

"Gotta run," he whispered.

Yes, he did. From the look on Crystal's face, she'd catch him, skates or not.

"But I'll see you at eight, okay?" he added.

Almost before she nodded, he was gone.

Jackson's mother continued smiling for the cameras, clasping Crystal in a firm grip.

Sadie put her fingers to her mouth and let loose a deafening whistle. "Way to go, Mrs. Cross! Way to go!"

Liz joined in.

20

At coffee hour back at the inn, Liz consoled Wayne and Chuck—especially Chuck—for their fifth- and seventh-place finishes in the men's snowmobile race. Sending a dozen oatmeal-raisin cookies along with her farewell brightened the guys' expressions considerably.

Liz also celebrated Bunny's first-place victory in the women's snowmobile race and Izzy's surprise third-place finish. Seeing the young woman's sparkling eyes and flushed cheeks, Liz hoped that accomplishment would help Izzy take small steps in looking to her future.

As Bunny's loaded semi pulled away, followed by Sofia's carful of Sunshine Sisterhood members, Liz waved from the front door. They answered with a chorus of shouted goodbyes and a blast of the semi's porch-shaking horn.

She'd miss these new friends but would see them again soon, as the Sunshine Sisterhood had pledged to visit and support Toni throughout her ordeal.

Finally, as she cleared up after coffee hour, Liz could focus on her own special evening.

The Sweetheart Dance.

After grabbing soup and a sandwich, she showered and fussed with her hair. Why did her locks always seem to become more obstinate when she wanted to look her best?

Eventually she coaxed it into cooperation, if not submission, with a pearl-and-rhinestone comb.

Liz gave herself a manicure and pedicure, then stepped into her sleek, midnight-blue dress. Turning in front of the mirror, she enjoyed its slimming effect once more. Tiny rhinestones sparkled in embroidered floral patterns on the right side of the dress, stretching from bodice almost to the hem. A knee-high slit accented the plain side. Matching chiffon fit perfectly from the sweetheart neckline to her throat and forearms. The comb, simple dangling earrings, and sparkling strappy heels worked well with the dress, as did her silver satin-and-rhinestone clutch.

When the front doorbell chimed, she texted Jackson. *These heels make me slow. Come on in.*

She truly didn't want him to stand out in the cold, but she also wouldn't mind witnessing the look on his face when she made a grand entrance. She heard the front door open, waited a beat, then moved out to meet him.

Liz almost giggled when she saw Jackson in the rotunda. He resembled a prom date, eyes round with awe, holding a gorgeous cluster of white roses held together with a silver ribbon.

Then he morphed into the man of any woman's dreams. Jackson could have graced international photo shoots. The tuxedo's coat fit closely over his broad shoulders and tapered to his narrow waist. An understated silver-gray vest and tie accented his handsome face and thick hair. And that smile . . .

Blink, girl. Breathe. Don't trip like this is your first time in heels.

As she reached the landing, Jackson took her hand. "Liz, you're an absolute vision."

"Thank you. You look wonderful too."

"I asked Mary Ann about your dress. I hope you like the corsage." He slipped the fragrant roses over her hand onto her wrist.

"It's perfect."

Liz shielded the lovely flowers as Jackson helped her with her elegant wool cape. As he walked her down the front sidewalk, she halted midstep. "Did you buy a new car?"

The charcoal-gray Lexus surprised her almost as much as Cinderella's carriage would have.

"No, I rented it for this special night." Jackson grinned as he opened its door with a bow. "It's a good thing I'd already thought of it. When Mom quizzed me about details for tonight, she said she'd have locked me in the bathroom rather than let me escort you in my truck, or even my sedan."

Liz marveled at how far Mrs. Cross had come.

Driving downtown after a festival's close always inspired a little melancholy. The lighted booths, the constant bustle and buzz of the crowds, the fun events—all had vanished as if by the wave of a wand. Now, only the occasional car and glow of the old-fashioned streetlights lit the quiet night.

Magic reappeared, though, as they pulled into the high school gym's drive. The main entrance had been transformed into a twinkly theater marquee. A uniformed doorman opened Liz's door, and Liz was surprised to see that it was Chief Houghton.

He touched his hat, then helped her out, smothering a whistle. "You two should be in the movies." The chief gestured to a red carpet sloping up to the front doors. "Have fun. You deserve it!"

After hanging up their coats, they joined others who exclaimed with delight as they walked through the foyer with its glowing lanterns and wintry, glistening decorations.

Entering the gym, however, struck them speechless.

Gone were the basketball goals, bleachers, scoreboards, and glaring lights of the typical Hoosier basketball season. Instead, draperies of tulle and soft white lights transformed the ceiling into a star-studded night sky. Clumps of bare-branched trees and evergreens covered with "snow," arrangements of mirrors, and more twinkling lights graced the big room. Scattered wrought-iron benches provided intimate spots where couples and friends could converse. A café full of white-covered tables, evergreen decorations, and candles surrounded a portable fireplace. On the opposite side of the gym, a tuxedoed band played for those already taking advantage of the beautifully lit dance floor.

Liz turned to Jackson. "Do you mind if we wander a little? I'd like to say hi and see everyone's dresses."

"Of course." He grinned. "I didn't understand that in high school, but I have learned a thing or two since then."

He bought cups of punch from the café, and they meandered toward the dance floor to greet friends.

At first, Liz didn't recognize Naomi, who had abandoned her all-American-girl look for a sparkly, off-the-shoulder, wine-red dress with sheer, fluttering sleeves. "You look gorgeous."

"So do you." Naomi's brown eyes, looking out from the dark waves of her messy French twist, twinkled with her usual smile. She introduced Evan, a fellow baker she'd met at a trade show. Attractive, with slightly funky glasses, he and Jackson seemed to click. In fact, Evan seemed to click with everyone he met—but with Naomi most of all. Liz loved seeing her quiet friend having such a good time.

The band erupted with their version of a pop song, which morphed the dance floor into a younger domain. Spotting Caitlyn proved easy. Her short, light-aqua dress featured a beaded bodice, with layers and layers of tulle forming the poufy skirt—a nightmare for some figures, but Caitlyn looked wonderful in it. Her date, Brice, who worked with her at the hospital, wore a tux that matched Caitlyn's dress. They danced at an energy level Liz couldn't imagine keeping up with, but loved to watch.

When the band toned down the next song, Jackson gestured toward the dance floor. "Since neither of us ended up in a body cast, would you like to dance?"

"I'd love to."

When his strong arm encircled her waist and pulled her close, Liz forgot about seeing the other women's dresses. Jackson moved to the music as if part of it, and she melted into its rhythms as well.

The song's end segued into another and another. The music held them together in its warm grasp.

A couple of swing numbers temporarily interrupted the spell as the oldest and youngest dancers gathered on the floor. Liz didn't mind too much—she and Jackson sipped lattes on the sidelines. They applauded Mary Ann and Sadie, wearing gray satin and bright pink respectively, who had come with the Senior Community Club. Mary Ann had brought her rarely seen husband, Howard, and Sadie had snagged a date from the club. Both men proved lively partners as the couples jitterbugged to "Chattanooga Choo-Choo" with almost as much get-up-and-go as Caitlyn and Brice.

They'd evidently persuaded Mrs. Cross to come as well. Sleek and stylish in a sage-green dress, she danced a graceful, more sedate step with local physician Dr. Sam Schneider.

Jackson grinned at Liz's expression. "Mom looks well, doesn't she?"

"Fabulous." Liz was delighted to see Mrs. Cross with a genuine smile. How wonderful to witness her having a good time in Pleasant Creek.

The surprise of the evening, however, proved to be Opal and George's waltz. George swept his wife, wearing a full-skirted, teal chiffon dress, across the floor with the grace and dexterity of Fred Astaire.

How did George, with his hearing challenges, stay with the music so well? Their moves were so elegant that most dancers paused to watch. Opal's cheeks turned rosy as a debutante's, but her smile told spectators how much she enjoyed this romantic interlude with her husband, perhaps reminiscent of their courtship decades before.

Jackson seemed to savor the sight as much as Liz. "They've loved each other so long and so well. Fun to watch, isn't it?"

When he turned to look at her, his expression sent heated shivers through her.

Suddenly, Jackson swept Liz out onto the dance floor with finesse equal to George's. They danced away the evening, letting the starlike glow of the lights and the magic of the music whirl them a galaxy away from the pressures and terrors of the previous weeks.

All too soon, they had to return to earth.

Finally, her weary bones told her it was time to go home. However, a late-night cup of herbal tea with Jackson might be nice. He agreed.

Jackson tucked her arm in his as they walked to the inn's front door. "Wouldn't want you to slip on the ice."

After removing his coat, Jackson put two logs on the fire in the sitting room while Liz brewed their tea.

After she set the cups on the coffee table, Jackson pulled her onto the settee beside him and took her hands. He took a deep breath. "Liz, you've been a dear friend through the best and worst of times. But I want us to be more than just friends." He peered into her face. "Are we, Liz?"

Liz struggled, then finally found her words. "Definitely more than friends, Jackson."

His warm lips found hers, and he kissed Liz with a tenderness and passion that electrified her.

When they finally separated, Jackson grinned. "There. I've been wanting to do that for ages."

Her mind had blanked, and the very air seemed to feed her dizziness. She finally managed to say, "I'm glad you didn't wait any longer. I think I'd like to try that again soon, Jackson." She touched his cheek. "Very soon."